A KISS FOR HOPE

A ROGUES TO RICHES HOLIDAY NOVELLA

GRACE BURROWES

GRACE BURROWES PUBLISHING

A Kiss for Hope

Cover design by Wax Creative, Inc.

To those for whom the holidays are challenging, which is probably all of us, sooner or later.

CHAPTER ONE

"Who in blazes are you, and where is Chumley?" Joshua Penrose kept his teeth from chattering as he posed his questions, but only just.

He pushed past the unfriendly female who'd opened the door to his dwelling and stomped into the dimly lit foyer. The house was cold —what English dwelling wasn't cold in December?—and faintly scented with balsam. Somebody had no doubt hung greenery where it ought not to be, a problem to be dealt with after Joshua's feet, face, and fingers thawed.

Assuming they ever did.

"I am Mrs. Hope Burdette, and I will thank you to take yourself out of my house this instant."

Mrs. Burdette was tallish for a woman and youngish for a housekeeper. She was clad in faded blue velvet skirts and two shawls, one black, one the same blue as the skirts. Both were ratty at the edges.

Fingerless black gloves completed this fetching ensemble, along with auburn hair scraped back into a bun. The scowl was imposing, or would have been were Joshua not exhausted past all bearing.

He closed the door and tossed off a bow. "Joshua Penrose." *At your service* would have been ridiculous. "I own the place. If you're the housekeeper, you work for me. I need a fire, if you please. Also a plate of victuals—sandwiches will do—and something hot to drink. Tea is acceptable—strong China black—but a toddy or chocolate would be welcome too. I trust there's a fire to be had somewhere?"

"What did you say your name is?"

Spare me from servants imbibing the holiday punch. "Joshua Penrose. I am your employer, though I've been on extended travel in the New World. We haven't met." He'd remember that chin, which hinted of determination and an opinionated aristocrat or two somewhere higher up on the family tree. Swooping brows went with an unapologetic nose and a well-defined jaw.

Cobwebs, dust, and lackadaisical underlings would stand no chance with this lady.

Mrs. Burdette was far from pretty, but she was attractive. She had substance and presence, and—Joshua would bet his share of the bank on this—an impressive temper.

"Mr. Penrose—if that is your name—I know not what scheme you are trying to hatch, but my husband purchased this house two and a half years ago. He paid dearly for it, and if you think to swindle me out of my home by dark of night and in the dead of winter, you have taken leave of your senses."

Feeling was flooding back into Joshua's extremities. An infernal itching joined exhaustion, hunger, and the crushing sadness he'd not managed to heave overboard during three weeks at sea.

"Any scheme, madam, must be yours. I have not sold this dwelling, nor have I authorized its sale. If you will produce your husband, I will happily acquaint him with the pertinent facts."

Joshua could see his breath in the shadowy foyer, and it absolutely was *his* foyer. He had not stumbled into the wrong house. The portrait over the sideboard was of *his* grandpapa, who'd had the house built as London's push away from the old walled City had gained momentum in the previous century.

The carpet was a fading Axminster woven to order for Joshua's grandmama. The corridor beyond would boast seascapes, landscapes, and a few exquisite botanical sketches, while the library doubled as a personal art gallery.

And, please heaven, might there be a lit fire in that library.

"Mr. Penroses, this is my house. I will thank you to vacate it at once." Mrs. Burdette pointed to the door, her other hand on her hip. "Now."

I am too tired for this. I am too angry for this. "Pen*rose.* Perhaps it has escaped your notice that the snow is coming down better than an inch to the hour. I had to walk half the distance from the docks because the hackneys are all taking the shelter any sensible creature should seek on a night like this. I have traveled thousands of miles, Mrs. Burdette, and I will not be turned away from my own doorstep to perish in truly dangerous weather."

The Joshua Penrose who'd left England all those years ago would never have addressed a woman, much less a female employee, so sternly. But then, he'd thought to spend only a few months in the former colonies before setting sail for home.

"The Wood and Willow will remain open until the end times," Mrs. Burdette retorted. "They are two streets over. For a few pints, they'll let you have a chair by the hearth for the night. I am a decent woman, and this is a decent house, and you will not impose yourself upon it."

"What happened to the Owl and Ocelot?"

She gathered her shawls more closely. "The daughter took over from her parents and changed the name. She claimed nobody knows what an ocelot is."

"I know what a winter storm is," Joshua said, "and that weather will take lives this night. If you can't be troubled to find me some comestibles, might we at least have this argument somewhere warmer?"

Another hitching up of the tattered shawls. "I'd rather not admit you to my house. Surely you grasp the proprieties involved?"

Mrs. Burdette was living up to the promise of her chin, drat and blast her. "I grasp that no sane creature is abroad in this weather, that mine were the only footprints in the increasingly deep snow for the length of three streets, and that anybody who has dwelled in these surrounds for more than five years will acknowledge that I have every right to be here."

"You've been away *five years?*"

"Longer, in fact, but right now, all I want is warmth and something to drink. You needn't feed me. I've been hungrier." If Joshua were any wearier, he'd be asleep on his feet, a perilous state of affairs on London's increasingly frigid and deserted streets.

"All well and good for you, sir, but what will the rest of the neighbors think about me, hailing a strange man in off the street, showing him hospitality he has not earned, and—"

"Mama, is he really a *stranger?*"

Joshua had to drop his gaze below the top of the sideboard. A small child had intruded on the conversation, as small children were wont to do. A female child goggled at Joshua with big, blue eyes. Her hair was coppery compared to her mother's auburn, and the girl's tresses were arranged in two unraveling plaits. Alas for the child, she also had her mother's chin.

"I am not a stranger." In this one house in this one city, Joshua Penrose was not a stranger.

"If you were," the girl said, "you might be an angel unawares. Are you sure you're not a stranger? 'Be not forgetful to entertain strangers: for thereby some have entertained angels unawares.' I've never seen a regular angel or an angel unawares."

"Hollister Ann Burdette, *where are your slippers?*"

The daft child was barefoot. Her robe looked snug enough, and she wore a flannel nightgown beneath, but her bare little toes had to be half frozen.

"I'm Holly," the girl informed Joshua. "Mama calls me Hollister Ann only when she's *zasperated* with me."

Joshua felt a compulsion to close his eyes and leave them closed just for a moment. To have a nice little lean on the sideboard for a few days' worth of nap. When he woke up cozy and warm in bed, he'd smell fresh bread baking, and one tug of the bedroom bell-pull would result in strong tea and a hot breakfast.

Not too much to ask, but at present, a complete fantasy.

He scooped up Hollister Ann and perched her on his hip. With his other hand, he hefted his satchel.

"Mrs. Burdette, I am growing a bit zasperated myself. If you would please lead the way to some warmth, I will entertain every argument you or your husband care to make, provided we first put some stockings and slippers on this child's feet."

Mrs. Burdette sniffed in the manner of a mama who knew she was being cozened. She collected the lit carrying candle from the sideboard and marched off down the corridor.

Joshua followed more slowly.

The seascapes needed a good cleaning, the runner was threadbare, and a decent landscape of Chatsworth was no longer hanging in its appointed location. A drawing of a child had taken its place, probably the same little sprite using the collar of Joshua's greatcoat as a teething rattle.

"What have you done with Chatsworth?" Joshua asked as Mrs. Burdette lifted the latch on the study door.

"I beg your pardon?"

"His Grace of Devonshire's ancestral pile. Immortalized in oils. Across from the pier glass." Which had acquired a few speckles near the bottom corners.

"You refer to a painting?"

"I do." Joshua expected that Mr. Burdette was to be found in the study, and surely that good fellow could be made to see reason. Morning was soon enough to sort out whatever misunderstanding—or swindle—had resulted in Mrs. Burdette's mistaken conclusions.

"Sold." She pushed open the door and admitted Joshua not to his study, but to a sort of parlor-cum-playroom where his study should have been.

The room was warm in comparison to the foyer, though any resemblance to Joshua's study ended there.

"Where is my desk?" A beautiful behemoth of carved oak, at least two hundred years old. Had drawers within drawers, at least three secret compartments, and was of a size for somebody of Joshua's height. "I love my desk. Please tell me that hasn't been sold as well."

"You love a *desk*?"

"My grandfather loved that desk too. An abacus was built into a panel on the righthand side. It pulls out, and you can... Yes, I love that desk." He did not love the slurping sound the child made right near his ear. She was very solid as sprites went. Heavier by the moment, in fact.

"A monstrosity of a desk occupies the alcove past the warming pantry."

"A beautiful monstrosity." By contrast, a plain, anemic little escritoire was angled by the fire. Joshua could smash that paltry excuse for furniture with one fist, and the idea gave him pleasure.

At least there *was* a fire, and a decent blaze at that. "Where is Mr. Burdette?"

He wasn't in this all-wrong room. A stuffed horse-ish creature on wheels sat near the window, complete with what looked like real horsehair for the mane and tail. A card table was positioned under the other window, sporting a chess set ready for play.

Where to put the...? Joshua draped the girl into a wing chair. She curled up immediately, her cheeks working as if her thumb were in her mouth.

Bare feet, of all the ridiculous... "About Mr. Burdette. If he's asleep at this hour, I suggest you do not disturb him. Morning will arrive in due course, and that's soon enough to resolve our misunderstandings. I will be happy with any guest room that boasts a fire."

The itching was subsiding, leaving Joshua with cold feet in damp, possibly ruined, boots.

"Mr. Burdette enjoys the eternal slumber of the just. You might as well have a seat. I was about to put the kettle on."

Mrs. Burdette spared the child one look that held both affection and despair, then decamped.

Tea was better than nothing. A warm dry sofa was a great improvement over numbing cold and frozen extremities. Joshua removed his greatcoat and tucked it around the dozing child, taking care to cover those impossibly vulnerable little feet.

He sat to remove his boots and had to pause—sitting—to clear his head.

"A bit muzzy." He removed both boots and his wool stockings, though that effort left him muzzier still. The carpeted floor was frigid, of course, so he pulled a hassock over to the sofa, unfolded the knitted blanket hanging over the back of the second wing chair, and tried to make five feet of blanket suffice for more than six feet of chilly man.

As a younger fellow, he might have found the situation comical. Perhaps in the morning, he'd be able to smile about it.

Not likely. He hadn't done much smiling for the past year.

He gave up on the hassock idea, curled up in a corner of the sofa, and got as much of himself under the blanket as he could manage. The last thought in his mind before sleep crashed over him like an avalanche was that putting Grandpapa's desk in an alcove was an abomination against the natural order, as any sensible body ought to have known.

~

Hope knew the look of a person coping on no sleep, no resources, and no joy. Mr. Penrose, despite his height and rudeness, fit the description. The shadows under his eyes looked like bruises, his cheekbones were too prominent, and his fair hair was in need of a trim. His tailoring was excellent, but everything from his greatcoat to his boots was looser than it should have been.

Hope's guest enunciated carefully, as if making thoughts audible took concentration when he yearned only for silence.

Hope knew that yearning. Sometimes, when Holly could not stop chattering, silence loomed as the only boon worth begging for. Mr. Penrose craved quiet. Hope knew that about him instinctively, and she knew he'd been telling the truth about tromping London's streets. A fine pair of boots had suffered a soaking in the snow, something only a desperate or heedless man would have allowed.

"If he even is Joshua Penrose," Hope muttered.

The pantry mouser opened his eyes and yawned. He was a fat-headed black-and-white specimen who wore a perpetual scowl that hid a sweet nature. Holly had named him Heifer, despite being well aware that a heifer was a female bovine. When Holly made up her mind, the celestial powers could not unmake it.

Much like her father.

Hope lowered the pot swing so the kettle was closer to the coals and considered whether she could spare some cheese toast. The cat was passionately fond of cheese. So was Holly.

"This fellow might be impersonating Mr. Penrose." Hope had to admit that he had a Penrose sort of beak, if the portrait in the foyer was any indication. The solicitors said the old fellow in the foyer had been a banker of some renown in the last century. There was still a financial institution carrying the Penrose name.

"Joshua Penrose has waited quite a while to run his rig, if he's an impostor."

People grew desperate as the holidays approached. The year's accounts would soon have to be paid, the worst of the cold still lay ahead, and in many trades, winter wages were hard to come by.

"A few slices won't matter." Hope warmed the teapot and filled it half full, then measured out exactly half a pot's worth of tea from the nearly empty drawer. While the tea steeped, she made two bread-and-cheese sandwiches and warmed them carefully on Edwin's sandwich toaster.

His contraption was two flat pieces of one-inch wire mesh hooked together with a toasting fork for the handle. Edwin had been certain he'd invented every kitchen maid's fondest dream, but nobody had been willing to pay for the idea. Why not just use the toasting fork for its intended purpose? One slice at a time was plenty efficient enough.

The pantry boasted some shortbread, courtesy of Mrs. Ingleby, but Hope saved that for Holly. With Christmas around the corner, Holly was trying so hard to be good, and mostly succeeding.

Hope assembled the tea tray—her last two matching cups, as it happened. Half a cream pitcher of milk—no cream had graced the kitchen since Edwin's demise—and a small bowl of irregularly shaped sugar lumps.

The cat gave her a reproving look when she lifted the tray, which was just too rubbishing bad.

"Eat a mouse, you fraud." Heifer hadn't caught a mouse in weeks, probably because that would require leaving the warmth of the hearth and actually doing some work.

He sat up tall and wrapped his tail about his paws, very much on his injured dignity.

"Drat you." Hope tore a tiny crumb of melted cheese from the corner of a sandwich and dropped it on the hearth at Heifer's paws. He fell to, and without so much as a hint of thanks.

Hope left him to it—that might be the last cheese Heifer enjoyed for quite some time—and braved the frigid house and shadowed corridors. Candles were dear, coal was dear, everything was dear.

Some memories were dear, and selling this house would make it harder to hold on to them.

But much easier to keep body and soul together. Hope balanced the tray on her hip, lifted the latch on the study door, and executed the half-sidling maneuver that opened the door to the least degree necessary for the shortest possible time.

Warmth was very dear.

"I've brought..."

Holly was fast asleep under acres of toasty wool, courtesy of Mr. Penrose's caped greatcoat. He'd taken care to cover her feet and to tuck the coat into the creases of the cushions lest Holly awake shivering.

Mr. Penrose himself was curled against the corner of the sofa, half slouching, arms folded, his bare feet peeking out from beneath Edwin's imagining afghan. Some people had considering caps to foster productive thoughts. Edwin had wrapped himself in an imagining afghan.

Hope touched the top of one of those big feet before propriety could stifle maternal pragmatism. The only thing worse than an unwanted houseguest at the holidays was an unwell unwanted house guest.

Ice-cold feet. He truly had walked half the length of London. Would a swindler bother to do that? Would he surrender his coat to keep a child warm?

She built up the fire, held her black shawl up before the leaping blaze, and when the wool was warm, wrapped it around those two large, pale feet. Mr. Penrose was by no means any sort of angel, but he was a stranger, and he was exhausted and hungry.

Even for the sake of respectability, Hope would not turn him away in the middle of a cold, dark, snowy night.

CHAPTER TWO

"Fear not: for, behold, I bring you good tidings of great joy, which shall be to all people and also to Heifer!"

Joshua ignored the daft voice in his head and clung to sleep with the determination of the utterly weary. If he awoke, he'd have to move, and think, and—worst of all—leave the blessed, blessed warmth of covers gently scented with balsam.

Was there ever a more pleasing, soothing scent?

"In this day in the city of London," the voice trumpeted on, "Mama is making breakfast, and unto us fried toast and bacon will be given!"

Something soft swatted Joshua's temple.

"I am the angel of the kitchen. You aren't supposed to ignore me."

He opened gritty eyes and beheld the girl—Hollister Ann of zasperation fame—standing on the rug. She had what looked like an old table linen wrapped around her shoulders, possibly in dubious homage to angel wings. In her hand was a copper soup ladle. She wore thick slippers, and equally sturdy black wool stockings covered her legs.

"I am the troll of the sofa," Joshua growled, "and I am asleep. I eat noisy little girls for breakfast." Joshua wasn't sure what fried toast was, but the idea of bacon made his belly rumble.

Then too, nature was calling him rather urgently.

"You are not a troll. You are a stranger. Mama says you have come from a land far away. Did you bring gold, frankincense, or more?"

"Myrrh. It's a tree sap with medicinal properties, and no, I did not. I brought a satchel."

The child reached around the end of the sofa and presented Joshua with his kit. "Mama says there's more snow on the way, and somebody had best clean your boots before they are ruined. I don't know how to clean boots."

Joshua did. "Please tell your mother that I will present myself in the kitchen posthaste, but must make my morning ablutions first."

Holly considered his now dry and water-stained boots. "You want to have a wash?"

"Among other things."

"The privy is at the foot of the garden. Mama says that's where all the best privies are found. We wash in the kitchen because that's the only other warm place in the house. Bye!"

She tapped him gently on the shoulder with her soup ladle and whirled out the door.

Joshua rose and earned aches and pains for his effort. His shoulders were sore, his hips positively creaky, and his left knee—he'd fallen on some slippery cobbles—was doubtless sporting a bruise.

The snow hadn't stopped but had slowed to flurries drifting down from a low, dark sky. The winter sky in London was always dark, something Joshua hadn't missed. The New World had forests in unimaginable abundance and was less dependent on coal as a result.

For now.

Joshua pulled on his abused boots and made the trek to the privy. The garden itself was draped in a foot of snow, the sundial sporting a conical cap of white. The crushed-shell paths were mere indications between the remains of herbaceous borders bowed down with snow.

Frigid. Bleak. He'd described the garden in detail to Maureen, but not in its present state. The bluebells carefully nurtured in the dappled shade of the aspen, the roses climbing the east-facing wall, the Holland bulbs announcing spring...

His feet were already cold again by the time he returned to the house. He nonetheless took a cursory tour of the lower floor and found Grandpapa's desk in the alcove. The great icon of Penrose family industry sat exposed to the dust and mice without so much as a linen shroud to mourn its lowered station.

Were Joshua inclined to moods, he'd say the sight of that beautiful, venerable testament to human skill and workmanship collecting dust in a cold corner annoyed him.

Fortunately, he was too tired, still, to be annoyed. Had been too tired since Maureen's passing. He presented himself in the kitchen, lured by the scent of frying bacon.

"We'll need a path shoveled clear along the garden walkway," Joshua said, relishing the warmth to be found nearest the enormous stone hearth. "More snow on the way means the job will only get harder."

Mrs. Burdette had donned a half-length white apron over her blue dress. She turned the bacon with the deft skill of an accomplished cook. "The shovel is in the gardener's shed. Good morning, Mr. Penrose. I hope you slept well."

He deserved that. Maureen would have chided him for his surly manners—and then kissed him out of them. "Good morning." Because the child was present and listening to every word, Joshua bestirred himself to *try*. "The bacon smells wonderful."

"Doesn't it, though? That disgrace to the feline species on the hearth is Heifer. He will pester you without end if you give him so much as a crumb. Holly spoils him shamelessly."

"So does Mama," Holly said, gathering her wings about her like a shawl and perching on the raised hearth. "Papa spoiled him most of all, and Heifer is still mad that Papa isn't here."

Holly was doubtless angry at her father for leaving the earthly realm. Joshua did not begrudge the child one iota of her outrage.

The cat had the black-and-white coat pattern of the pied cattle of the Low Countries and Northern Germany. His purr could be heard across the kitchen, and his dignity had gone begging as soon as Holly commenced scratching his head.

"I don't care for cats in the normal course."

"Then you must enjoy having mice in your pantries," Mrs. Burdette replied. "Heifer isn't much of a mouser, but even having him on the premises serves as a deterrent to rodents." She shifted her attention to a second skillet, where pieces of bread dipped in some sort of batter were frying. "Holly, you must wash your hands before you come to the table."

They were apparently to eat in the kitchen. A workbasket suggested Mrs. Burdette did her mending in here, and a stack of books on the scarred table hinted that the kitchen was doing extra service as a schoolroom.

Why didn't Hollister Ann have a governess? Where were the footmen and maids? And what had become of old Chumley?

"I could do with a basin and towel myself," Joshua said, though the request felt awkward. The basins were in the butler's pantry, the towels in the laundry. "Why don't I see to that?"

"Good idea," Mrs. Burdette said. "Holly would take it very much amiss if I burned her fried toast, and Heifer would not speak to me until spring if I overcooked the bacon."

The lady, in other words, was *busy*.

Joshua collected a basin, poured some hot water into it from the kettle on the hob, and added cold water from a pitcher in the sink. He retreated to the laundry—a frigid, gloomy space that nonetheless had towels and a few tins of soap—and set about getting clean before his teeth started chattering.

A near thing, though not entirely unpleasant. Getting clean was always a pleasure, and even the soap smelled of balsam.

By the time he returned to the kitchen, his brain had started working, and the evidence all around him had coalesced into a conclusion: Mrs. Burdette and her angel-in-training were squatting in his house because the lady was in want of coin. This reality penetrated his thinking as it hadn't the previous night. Of course, the average confidence trickster was short of the ready, but one didn't associate frying bacon and motherhood with confidence tricksters.

If Mrs. Burdette was a lady, her fall onto hard times had happened some while ago. She had been without adequate coin long enough to think like a poor person. To make any space serve as many purposes as possible, just to conserve coal. To casually inform one of the wealthiest bankers in the realm that he'd have to shovel his own way to the privy.

A bit of irony there. A touch of humor, even.

Joshua retrieved his shaving kit from his satchel and returned to the chilly shadows of the laundry. As he went through the ritual of scraping whiskers from his cheeks, his thoughts circled back to Mrs. Burdette.

She was wearing the same dress she'd had on the previous day, and even in her kitchen, the only real warmth, the only place that approached cozy, was the space immediately before the hearth.

How dare she be desperately poor and under Joshua's very roof when he needed solitude and quiet? How dare she keep her late husband's ugly cat when it could not be bothered to pull his weight?

"Holly likes him," Joshua informed his reflection. "That cat is nobody's fool."

Joshua was looking less like a bit of human flotsam cast up on the tide when he rejoined the ladies in the kitchen, but he felt just as unsettled as when he'd arrived to his own home to find Mrs. Burdette in her two tattered shawls.

"Have a seat," she said, putting a plate in front of him. "We do not stand on ceremony when hot food is to be consumed. Holly, rinse your hands. You may say the blessing."

The girl ceased splashing in a basin at the sink, dried her hands on an apron hanging from a peg on the crossbeam, and skipped over to the table.

"For what we are about to receive," she said, wiggling onto the bench beside Joshua, "we are very, very grateful, and God bless the fall heifers and our Heifer too."

A most unusual grace. "Why the fall heifers?" Joshua asked. Meaning the bovines who freshened in autumn.

"Butter," Holly replied, her little features earnest. "Butter for the bread and the toast and the spuds and butter, butter, butter. Heifer likes butter too."

"Is butter good for him?" Did the cat have no sense of his place in creation?

"We don't know, so we never give him more than a tiny, tiny dab to lick at, but his name is Heifer, so he should like butter. Mama, may I have a lump?"

Mrs. Burdette arranged herself across from her daughter on the opposite bench. "You may have one. Mr. Penrose might like to sprinkle his toast with a bit of sugar as well."

"The French call this dish *pain perdu*—lost bread," Joshua said as Holly stared intently at the bowl of lump sugar. "Probably because stale bread works as well as fresh. Child, what are you about?"

"Mama said one lump, so I'm looking for the biggest one. That's fair."

"You may have my lump as well," Joshua said, then realized he'd just countermanded a maternal order, which the slowest step-papa soon learned he was never to do. "Provided your mother agrees."

"Mama?"

"You may have the top two lumps in the bowl if you thank Mr. Penrose for sharing."

"Thank you, Mr. Penrose, and happy Christmas too!" The wonder in Holly's eyes as she pinched the lumps to sugar dust and sprinkled them on her toast made Joshua uncomfortable.

"You're not having any sugar?" he asked Mrs. Burdette.

"I prefer mine plain." She also preferred to consume her toast in tiny, savored bites, eaten in a slow progression.

Not simply in want of coin, then, but destitute. She also consumed her weak tea plain—the leaves were probably reused from last night's pot—and she ate only one strip of bacon, while serving two to the girl and three to Joshua.

Even a confidence trickster deserved adequate tucker. Joshua put his third strip of bacon on her plate.

"I am not that fond of bacon," he said, "but good food shouldn't—"

"Go to waste!" Holly bellowed.

"Thank you."

Something about the genuine humility of Mrs. Burdette's reply left Joshua thinking that she was indeed a lady fallen on hard times. Very hard, if a born lady turned confidence trickster.

The rest of the meal passed in the sort of busy quiet that springs up when hungry people are intent on dispatching food.

"What's for lunch?" Holly asked when her plate had not a morsel left upon it. "Should I look in the conservatory for more eggs?"

"Eggs in the conservatory?" Grandpapa's conservatory was not a henhouse.

"Mrs. Bennifer keeps her hens in our conservatory when she goes to the country for the holidays," Mrs. Burdette explained. "There's enough light that the hens do occasionally lay, and we keep the eggs in exchange for minding the biddies. We found two eggs yesterday, Holly, so today we aren't likely to find any."

Mrs. Burdette had made a meal out of two eggs, a dash of milk, and some stale bread.

Holly set her plate aside. "I shall look anyway. Christmas is the season of miracles. I might find a golden egg!"

"Then bundle up first, and don't let Heifer follow you in. The hens pick on him terribly."

"May-I-be-excused-and-thank-you-for-breakfast, Mama." Holly was off the bench and out the door, her wings once more pressed into service like a shawl.

"Her manners are a work in progress." Mrs. Burdette rose and collected Holly's dishes and utensils. "A very slow work in progress some days. She wants to find eggs to impress you, but I'm afraid..."

Mrs. Burdette paused at the sink, her back to Joshua. For him to sit at the table while she labored at the sink was... Maureen would have disapproved.

Joshua rose and collected the rest of the dishes. "You are afraid?"

"Before I could procure comestibles for today's lunch, I'd have to sell something, or somebody would have to pay me for services rendered—several customers are past due—and with the snow, I don't see that happening. I've maybe three slices of bread left, thin slices at that, and a bit of cheese, but not much else in the larder."

She worked as she spoke, putting dishes into the lukewarm water Holly had used to wash her hands, pouring a bit of hot water into the skillets still on the stove.

"I can wash," Joshua said. "One doesn't forget how. You are telling me the food has run out?"

"Very nearly. Last winter by about February we were in the same condition. I am an ineffective debt collector, and to sell Edwin's things is difficult when they would bring so little coin. The solicitor was very clear that I ought not to sell the fungibles in the house, because I'll get a better price for the place if I can sell it looking spruce and luxurious."

As it had looked when Joshua had dwelled within its walls.

He scrubbed the first plate, trying to concoct an accusation. Something along the lines of this pathetic story would not move him to relent on the matter of the house, and Mrs. Burdette ought to be ashamed of herself for plucking so heartlessly at Joshua's nonexistent heartstrings.

Et cetera and so forth.

The woman was thin. Without her shawls and by the decent light of the kitchen, she was nearly gaunt.

"What services do you sell?"

"I take in mending, of course. I will also stitch samplers to order—they make nice holiday tokens—and I can teach servants to read. When my wealthier neighbors decamp for the shires at Yuletide and close up their houses, I water their plants, leave a dish of milk out for the cats, and so on. I will do any honest work I can find, but one doesn't… That is… I am not… I don't find much."

The simple solution would be for Joshua to send to the bank for a draft and write this woman and her child out of his life. Sending to the bank would alert Quinn to Joshua's return, though, and Joshua was not yet ready to face that gauntlet.

The even simpler solution would be to pull some coins from his own pocket and trot around to the chophouse, where good, plain fare was available in abundance.

"I haven't any coin either," Joshua said. "One doesn't use coin on board ship, and American coin isn't British coin, and what British coin I do have is with my luggage." He might have tossed a few pennies into his satchel at some point.

"In this weather, no telling when your luggage will arrive."

And one could not even send a message to the docks without coin for the messenger or ticket porter.

The simplest solution of all popped into Joshua's head as he was rinsing off a tea cup. "The shovel is in the gardener's shed?"

"At least one, possibly more."

"Then start planning your luncheon menu." He passed over the tea cup for Mrs. Burdette to dry. "God knows I can wield a shovel."

"You'd labor like that?"

"I need to eat, you and your child need to eat, and sooner or later the coal will also run out. Coin becomes a priority."

"We have enough coal for one more week." She set the tea cup on the towel where the rest of the dishes were drying. "If you're going out and about, you'll need old boots. Edwin's should fit you. I haven't been able to sell them. They still do the job, but they're a bit worn."

That Joshua was proposing to shovel snow to keep Mrs. Burdette and her offspring in bread and butter should have astonished him. She was the next thing to a thief, and the sooner she and Holly were off to some charitable establishment, the better.

Though the charitable establishments were rife with disease, and the house would have been standing empty were she not here.

Joshua accepted the loan of a pair of sturdy, worn boots, donned his greatcoat, gloves, and scarf, and collected the gardener's flat shovel.

He would sort out Mrs. Burdette and her mendacious claim to the house later.

If he wanted any kind of meal in the next day or two, the time to take advantage of London's snowy streets was now.

~

To Joshua's surprise, an army of boys had beaten him to the job. Some wielded brooms fashioned from bundled twigs, two had dustpans, and several others had dilapidated shovels.

"You can't work here, mister. This is our patch." One of the taller shovel-wielding fellows gestured grandly as if indicating the entire street.

"This is my front door," Joshua replied, "and I haven't given you leave to set foot on my property. That makes you trespassers." A very broad—and erroneous—reading of the law as it applied to London walkways.

The boys had made minimal progress with their makeshift tools. At least three members of this ragged regiment were barely out of leading strings, and one boy's toes were visible through the holes in his boots.

Calculation came into the taller boy's eyes. He was doubtless assessing Joshua's diction, the value of his greatcoat, the quality of the lamb's-wool in his black scarf.

"You dint *not* give us leave to be here, and we done a power of work already."

"You have created a greater mess, tramping the snow down and narrowing the walkway. Move aside. I'll show you how it's done."

With boys, establishing authority on some topic was imperative. The bank employed any number of young fellows. They would work loyally and well, provided their superiors had earned their respect.

Heaven help the manager who thought to maintain order in the junior ranks on the strength of age, size, and threats. Bullies had no place among the bank's junior ranks.

One of the smaller boys shifted to stand on the front steps, the rest followed.

Joshua made a quick, tidy job of shoveling off his own frontage. "Like that, so you don't have to shovel the same lot twice, and you don't make your job harder by packing the snow with your boots before you shovel it. Who wants to give it a try?"

He held up his shovel, and the spokesman snatched it. "I know me job, toff."

What the boy did not know was how it felt to push away from the table with a full belly. He was that thin. If he survived into adolescence, he'd be even thinner. Several inches of wrist and ankle showed, and his coat was held together with twine.

He made a good effort to extend the area Joshua had cleared, but he hadn't Joshua's strength or stamina.

"Well done," Joshua said. "Now, how about if I negotiate a price for finishing Mr. Clattermule's walkway?"

"Clattermule died," one of the smaller boys said through chattering teeth. "That's Hophouse's place now."

Ye gods. Clattermule hadn't been that old. "Then I will negotiate with the present resident."

"I will neg-oh-see-ate with the present re-si-dent," a boy with a dustpan said, sticking his nose in the air. "Give it a go, guv, and we'll laugh when the watch comes to haul you off to the bin."

Joshua had eaten a hot, if small, breakfast that included tea, albeit weak tea. He'd slept out of the weather, and he was intimately acquainted with money and its handling. These boys had likely never seen a genuine gold sovereign, and they'd be lucky to consume cold porridge once a day.

"Done," Joshua said, sticking out a gloved hand. Several of the boys shook, though not the leader. "And you,"—he tossed his gloves to the boy with holes in his boots—"put these on your feet. They'll do for stockings, and then you can sell them and get real stockings that fit."

"You don't want 'em back?" the boy said, fingering the gloves wonderingly.

The little boy who'd been first up the steps took the opening. "He won't want 'em back after they been on your smelly feet, Slivers."

The ambiguity of the riposte sent a fierce ache through Joshua's heart. Boys thrived on this sort of wayward diplomacy. What sounded like an insult was, in fact, a sop to a fellow's dignity. Smelly feet were a point of puerile pride, and deflecting the conversation from Slivers's poverty was pure kindness.

Even at a young age, Eric had known how to distract his playmates with a quip or a joke. His cheerful demeanor had been a gift from his mama, but that instinct, to take up in a sideways fashion for the boy who'd been left out or who'd become the butt of a taunt, had been Eric's alone.

The heartache passed, more slowly than Joshua would have wished, and he left the boys to debate who had the most odoriferous feet. Joshua rapped on what had been Mr. Stephan Clattermule's front door and found himself facing Riggs, who had been Clattermule's butler.

"Tradesmen around the back, my good man. Shouldn't have to tell you that."

He does not recognize me. That thought was lowering, also useful. "Around back is two feet deep in snow. These lads can shovel you out in the next half hour, front and back, if you can spare a bit of the household coin."

The butler looked past Joshua to the boys. His gaze then traveled up the walkway to the cleared patch in front of Joshua's house.

"They did Mrs. Burdette's walkway?"

Mr. Penrose's walkway. "In about a quarter hour and for a reasonable price." A short negotiation commenced. The butler was no match for one born with an abacus in one hand and a ledger in the other.

Joshua had no idea what the going rate for cleared walkways was, but the boys were impressed with his results. He rapped on another half-dozen doors while the boys fell to, and by the time he'd secured agreements with almost every house on the street, the coin was starting to pile up.

"Please, God, may it keep snowing forever," the tall boy said when Joshua informed him of the total the team stood to earn. "Who are you, anyway, mister?"

"I own property on this street. Used to live here. Name's Penrose." Joshua stuck out a hand, and this time, the boy shook.

"Gabriel. What do we owe you?"

They occupied the stone wall that separated the walkway from the small fenced square at one end of the street. Some obliging boy had broomed the snow off, leaving a penetrating cold in its place.

"Owe me?" Negotiating on behalf of the boys had been a small pleasure. A rusty skill put to modest use, yielding results that pleased both the boys and the households who'd bought their services.

"We couldn't never have charged what you got for us, and some of the smaller lads were just in the way until you showed them how to go on. Slivers needs proper stockings, or he'll lose his smelly toes. What do we owe you?"

"You would make a fine banker, Gabriel. You aren't afraid to discuss coin, and you appreciate the symmetry of a fair transaction."

Gabriel scratched his nose and gazed at the pewter sky. The boy had patience, another skill every competent banker claimed.

"I need enough coin for a loaf of bread, some cheese, a few apples, milk, and a couple days' worth of ham for three people."

"No gin? Gin comes cheap. Keeps you warm."

"No gin." For pity's sake, what had London come to? The boy might not have seen twelve years. "And I'll shovel for the next hour."

Gabriel grinned, his teeth surprisingly white in his grimy face. "No shirkin', Penrose. We're good lads. Not like some."

Meaning Gabriel wasn't picking pockets today. "No shirking."

Joshua reclaimed his flat shovel from one of Gabriel's minions and put in a good hour at a steady pace. When a snowball fight broke out among the lower ranks, he kept working and was declared to be no damned fun.

One did not tolerate insubordination, even if the charge was true.

As the accuser darted off across the street, Joshua fashioned some ammunition and potted the little beast on the shoulder. Work resumed in high spirits, and Joshua was almost sorry when Gabriel informed him that his hour-long indenture had been amply satisfied.

CHAPTER THREE

"I do not care for this." When Quinn Wentworth, known to the best society as His Grace of Walden, took a situation into dislike, his voice radiated his displeasure as clearly as a winter night crackled with cold. "I don't like this at all, Jane."

Her Grace of Walden, whom the duke esteemed exceedingly, was accustomed to her husband's moods and tempers. She was less adept at dealing with his worries, so thoroughly did he usually hide them from sight. She was learning, though. With each passing year of marriage, Jane felt closer to her husband and to the family she'd married into.

"Joshua might not have been on the ship," she said, topping up her tea cup. "He might have decided not to risk a winter passage after all."

Quinn sent a disgusted look at the window. "He promised me, Jane. Said he'd be here by the New Year. Why didn't I tell him that spring would suit? Why did I send him to the rubbishing New World to begin with?"

From worry to woe. The sitting room boasted a few cloved oranges hanging in the windows, and the ties holding back the burgundy velvet drapes had been decorated with sprigs of holly. The oranges and spice scented the room with a rich aroma Jane had always associated with Yuletide, and the snow drifting down outside should have been pretty.

Her Grace rose and moved around the sitting room to deposit herself in her husband's lap.

"You did not send Joshua to New York. He sent himself." Jane had a few theories as to why Joshua had banished himself. Of a certainty, opening a bank branch in New York had been shrewd business, but shrewd business could hide a multitude of more complicated personal motivations.

Quinn's arms came around her, and his chin rested against her temple. The sense of peace and safety Jane had found with her unlikely spouse still surprised her, still counted as one of her greatest blessings.

"Joshua did not send himself," Quinn rumbled. "He looked about, saw that his banking partner was newly besotted, and took a notion to absent himself. If he needed a respite, why not just go to Paris?"

"He went to New York because the Americans have money. Now we have some of their money, thanks to Joshua."

Quinn shifted, which allowed Jane to snuggle closer. Her husband always smelled good, no matter the hour of the day or season of the year. He was fanatic about his personal hygiene and immaculate in his dress. Years clawing his way up from the gutter had given the duke a focus on hygiene and attire that the Joshua Penroses of the world acquired by casual right of birth.

"Of course the Americans prosper," Quinn said. "They are a nation of unchecked thieves. Their papas and grandpapas stole fortunes from nearly every shop owner and manufactory in England."

Even for Quinn, that was bitter and exaggerated. "England lost the war, Quinn." Nearly two generations ago. "Victors generally dictate the terms, and some of the Americans did pay their British creditors."

"Damn few. The larger the debt, the less likely it was ever paid. Privilege of the peerage, American-style. A banker recalls these things. And I sent Joshua to deal with that lot."

Quinn was a superb banker, in part because he excelled past all bounds at carrying responsibility. For his family, for his customers, and certainly for the only man willing to throw in with him when the City itself was betting that Quinn's bank would fail.

"Joshua has managed quite well in New York," Jane said, kissing Quinn's cheek. "The bank will benefit enormously from the years he spent across the sea."

"Joshua did not benefit."

Jane rose. This was a topic they'd danced around for more than a year. "You don't know that, Quinn. If I was carried away by an ague tomorrow, would you regret having married me?"

Quinn was on his feet, Jane's hand seized in a warm grip. "Don't speak like that. Don't speak of the devil and draw him nigh. I could never, ever regret marrying you."

"But you assume Joshua regrets marrying his Maureen. His letters were ebullient, Quinn. Over the moon, rhapsodic, top over tail. He'd found his true love at long last and blessed the ship that had brought him to New York."

Quinn cradled Jane's hand against his cheek. To employees, competitors, or slacking tradesmen, he could be the most forbidding judge they ever encountered. When private with Jane, he was unfailingly affectionate.

"Joshua has likely since cursed his decision to leave England, assuming he didn't jump overboard."

Dark thoughts indeed, but then, Quinn had dwelled in hell and faced death on his way to the peerage. "Quinton Wentworth, what in the name of the herald angels put such morbid thoughts into your head?"

"He hasn't sent word of his arrival, has he? The snow was already a foot deep when his ship docked yesterday. He knows we expect him to spend the holidays with us, and yet... we have no idea where he is. If ever I lost you, Jane..."

"Joshua did not jump overboard. Winter makes you morose, Quinn. London boasts any number of comfortable inns where Joshua might have stayed."

"I hate winter." Quinn dropped Jane's hand and went to the window. A casual glance might miss the fact that it was even snowing, so fine were the flakes. Sneaky snow like this would add up by the hour.

"I am not fond of the darkness," Quinn said, "or the bitter cold. I am beyond intolerant of the forced joy of the holidays when, for many, the New Year will bring only hardship, or worse, no matter how many carols they sing in December. You do not want to be a banker in December, Jane. January is even worse."

Jane did not want to be a banker *ever*. "You feel responsible for Joshua's sorrow, but, Quinn, that matter was entirely out of your hands. Influenzas, agues, and lung fevers come every winter."

Jane joined him at the window and slipped an arm around his waist. She fit against him as she would never have fit a shorter man. Another blessing. Their physical compatibility was the outward symbol of a union of respect and affection that baffled most of Quinn's aristocratic peers. But then, Quinn himself was an enigma to them too.

He worked hard, he had no use for appearances, and he was devoted to his family. He was neither a jumped-up cit nor a haughty toff. He was simply Quinn Wentworth, and if Jane ever lost him...

What Joshua must be suffering, to have buried a spouse at the holidays. No wonder he'd left New York rather than suffer through another Yuletide in the house he'd shared with his true love.

"A double cruelty," Jane said, resting her head on Quinn's shoulder. "To lose a wife and to lose the joy of the holidays. We cannot expect him to be our old Joshua."

A rap on the sitting room door had Jane dropping her arm from

Quinn's waist. He was the duke, and his dignity, much less Jane's, required occasional concessions to decorum.

"Enter," Quinn growled.

Ned bounced through the door, cheeks ruddy, eyes alight, his dark hair damp with melting snowflakes. He was leaving boyhood behind and emerging into manhood with a sense of self-possession Jane would never have predicted of a former pickpocket. Ned wasn't the spectacular specimen Quinn was, but dear Neddy was quietly handsome, if Jane said so herself, and people found him easy to talk to.

"He's here," Ned said, grinning. "Penrose left the docks on foot, heading toward the City."

Thank heavens. "That is good news." Jane approached Ned and fussed his tousled dark hair. "The traveler is on home shores. We'll see him again soon."

"Or," Quinn said, "the traveler was set upon by footpads and has expired behind a ruddy snowbank. Good work, Ned, but please keep looking."

"We are, Your Grace. We won't stop until we find him. Penrose knows his way about Town, and we'll likely come across him being waited on hand and foot by some lucky innkeeper's daughters."

Ned departed at an exuberant pace, closing the sitting room door behind him unquietly.

"Ned is still at home on the streets," Quinn said. "We've taken the pickpocket out of Newgate, but a bit of the urchin remains."

"He's quite grown up, Quinn, and a fine testament to your guiding influence." And to Jane's unwavering patience. Ned had been infernally quick as a boy and absolutely incapable of sitting still.

"We're going to lose him," Quinn said, wrapping Jane in a loose hug. "He'll fall in love, and we'll lose him to some dairymaid or seamstress."

Quinn loved fiercely and forever. Jane adored that about him, but he had some odd notions about the particulars such devotion entailed. A loved one no longer needing protection left Quinn all at sea.

"The family will not lose Ned," Jane said. "We will gain a dairy-maid or seamstress. Honestly, Quinn. Must I order mistletoe hung from every lintel to improve your mood?"

His smile, always so warm and unexpected, held a hint of teasing. "Yes. Such measures will improve my mood significantly, though I will have to spend my days lurking in doorways."

"You awful man." Jane found herself challenged to an impromptu kissing match, which felt to her to be part mutual reassurance and part marital silliness.

"You know," Quinn said when combat had been fought to an honorable draw, "Joshua did not suffer a double cruelty. If we consider the child, the blow was treble, at least."

Jane had refrained from mentioning the boy, but Quinn never flinched in the face of difficult topics, another necessary quality in a banker.

"Awful blows, I agree," Jane said, "but Joshua is home now, and recovery from fate's buffeting is always easier with good friends about. I have it on the best authority that companionship in this life can make all the difference."

"Some duke or other told you that?"

"A grouchy banker. Come along, Quinn. I will need help hanging another two dozen sprigs of mistletoe."

Quinn came along, but Jane knew he would not be truly amenable to holiday cheer until Joshua Penrose was found, safe and sound.

~

Hope gave the candles one last dip, their balsam scent filling the kitchen. This was the final batch, and Hope worried that she'd left the making of them too late. The first few batches had sold well, but

Christmas was around the corner, and if bad weather kept people indoors until then, the last batch might not sell at all.

"When will Mr. Penrose come home, Mama?" Holly carefully folded a round piece of newsprint into quarters, then eighths. She'd been at her project for more than an hour, covering the worktable with the results of her handiwork and the floor with bits of paper.

"This is not his home, Holly. If he found more work, he might not be back for some time. He might also have decided to bide elsewhere." To give up on his house-swindling scheme, if any such scheme he'd had. As much as Holly wanted to attribute such mischief to him, Mr. Penrose seemed lacking in any capacity for mischief at all.

"But what about his *things*, Mama?" Holly took up Hope's cutwork scissors and began snipping. "His good boots are here and his satchel, and I am making snowflakes for him."

Which explained Holly's particular diligence, of course. "He'll send a ticket porter for his effects, if need be." With luck, Hope would never see him again.

The thought should have brought relief, except that Mr. Penrose had been intent on procuring food before he'd been swarmed by Gabriel's gang.

"If we made snowflakes out of linen," Holly said, "we could starch them, and then they would last forever."

"If we made snowflakes out of linen, they'd be harder to cut out and more expensive. We would have to content ourselves with three or four and not the vast snowbank you're making of *The Times*."

"My hands get dirty from the newspaper. Linen would not get my hands dirty." Holly held up her latest creation, a delicate octagon of more holes than paper. "When will Mr. Penrose be back?"

"I can't speak for him, but we might see him soon." The morning was gone, though the day was so gloomy that the sky gave no clue as to the hour as snow continued spitting down.

"Can we go out now that the candles are done? I've made enough snowflakes."

Holly had made dozens, with the same sort of patient focus her father had turned on one invention after another.

"A short constitutional only," Hope said. "The walkways are all but cleared, thanks to Gabriel and his friends, but the snow hasn't stopped." The cleared walkways were also thanks to Mr. Penrose. As best Hope had been able to tell, he'd organized the boys and let the neighbors know that a shoveling brigade was available for hire. Then he'd joined the ranks and done the lion's share of the work.

Kind of him, also shrewd.

"Is Gabriel a first name or a last name?" Holly added her latest creation to the stack on the mantel, where Heifer could not turn her hard work into playthings.

"I don't know which sort of name it is. You might ask him. It's a good name. Let's get into our boots." Hope was not going in search of Mr. Penrose—if he was gone, so much the better, really—but by dint of two hours' hard work by the parlor windows, she had a sampler to deliver.

On earth peace, goodwill toward men. Hope bore Mr. Penrose no goodwill whatsoever if he sought to steal the last asset she had to sell. Once the mortgage was cleared, the house wouldn't bring much, but some of the furnishings were valuable, and Hope had learned to live frugally.

"Are we looking for Mr. Penrose?" Holly asked when her boots were laced and her cloak wrapped around her.

"We are not. He is a grown man and can find his own way." Though London had probably changed a great deal during his absence, and travel was wearying. He might be lost.

"But what if he slipped in the snow and banged his head and doesn't know where he is?"

Hope wrapped Edwin's old scarf around Holly's neck. "You are fanciful. If he did not slip on snowy streets when he was navigating them by dark of night, he's unlikely to slip on cleared streets in broad daylight." Then too, Edwin's old boots were sturdy.

Mr. Penrose was not sturdy. He needed more meat on his bones, and he needed for that half-wild, distracted light in his eyes to fade.

"I wish we could go sledding."

Once when Holly had been four, Edwin had taken her sledding in the park. The memory had been trotted out with every snowfall since his death. Another reason to dislike snow.

"The snow is too deep for sledding, though many will have their sleighs out in the next few days. Where are your mittens?"

Holly extracted them from the pockets of her cape and pulled them on. They were too big for her, but warm enough for present purposes.

"Where are your mittens, Mama?"

Sitting in a shop window in Petticoat Lane. "My gloves will do if I keep my hands in my pockets. Let's be off, shall we?"

"And maybe we will find Mr. Penrose!" Holly clearly wanted to, but then, she had a trusting heart and few enough distractions in life. The thought of her in service, made to drudge fourteen hours a day, no fresh air, no impromptu walks... Hope would gladly take on that burden for herself if it meant Holly was provided for, but a little girl deserved better.

Perhaps Orson and Alma might relent, but surely it wasn't yet time to seek last resorts such as that?

We haven't much, but we still have authority over our time. A significant boon. Hope collected the finished sampler that she'd wrapped in newspaper and twine and prepared to be politely relentless.

Some enterprising soul had broomed off the area steps, another boon. Arriving to Mrs. Colchester's door with wet hems would have earned Hope a polite frown and a few disparaging comments about the weather taking a toll on fashion.

Mrs. Colchester would also frown at Holly and frown at the sampler. She would damn the latter with faint praise and the former with outright criticism, but if she paid in coin, Hope would count the outing successful.

"Mama, your hands aren't in your pockets. You should have worn your mittens."

"My hands are full of Mrs. Colchester's sampler. We'll deliver it while we're out and about, shall we?" No sign of Gabriel's minions or Mr. Penrose, though a few pedestrians were taking advantage of the passable walkway, and a lone sleigh glided up the street, bells jingling in rhythm with the trotting horse.

"I don't like Mrs. Colchester." Holly tried to catch a snowflake on her tongue. "She doesn't like me either."

"She is not the most warmhearted soul. I try not to judge her for that." Mr. Penrose wasn't warmhearted either, but Hope found his company easier to bear than Mrs. Colchester's.

Holly twirled on the walkway, tongue out, eyes closed. "I love snow."

"I love you." Loved the girl's energy, joy, and curiosity, even as all those qualities also frequently left a mama exhausted and bewildered.

"Love you too, Mama. Will Mr. Penrose be home when we get back?"

"I don't know." He came from means, based on the quality of his attire and his public school diction, except that he hadn't had sufficient coin to buy a loaf of bread. "We might not see him again, Holly."

"That's not fair. He came from the east, and he's a stranger, and he came bearing gifts."

"What gifts?" An eviction notice was not a gift. He could not legally evict them—only the bank could do that—but widowhood had given Hope a rapid, disconcerting education on how cold the comfort of legalities could be.

"He shoveled our walkway and got Gabriel's troupe to do the rest. That's a gift."

Probably as great a gift to Gabriel and his little thieves as it was to the neighborhood. "I want to think well of Mr. Penrose, but we don't know him, Holly." An echo of the same criticism Hope had faced when accepting Edwin's suit: *But, my dear, we don't know who his people are.*

Even wanting to think well of Mr. Penrose was a problem, but widowhood had also disabused Hope of the habit of self-deception.

"I do think well of him, Mama." Holly stopped at the foot of Mrs. Colchester's steps. "I do not think well of Mrs. Colchester. She only pretends to put pennies in the poor box."

Hope had seen that little ruse. Mrs. Colchester would make a quiet show out of fishing in her coin purse for tuppence and then examine the specimen she found before brushing her gloved hand over the slot in the top of the poor box. Close scrutiny saw the coin returned to the purse as soon as Mrs. Colchester enjoyed the safety of her pew.

She knelt while replacing the coin in her purse, the better to hide her miserliness.

"Mrs. Colchester is a widow," Hope said, staring up at a door graced by a wreath Hope had made herself. "She must be mindful of her coin, and she's probably worried that she'll be judged for not being able to make a contribution."

Mrs. Colchester had the funds to make a regular donation, but she lacked the requisite generosity of spirit.

"I will tell her to pay you, Mama. You made a very pretty sampler with doves and roses and everything."

"That won't be necessary, but thank you." The part of Hope's heart that was still prone to wishes and wondering begged providence to deliver her from the next quarter hour. "Holly, you remember the rule?"

"Seen and not heard. I'll be good, Mama."

And the child would earn stale shortbread for her virtue. "I will be good too." Try to be, but meek gratitude for a pittance here and there was becoming harder and harder to make convincing.

"Mama! It's Mr. Penrose!"

Holly spun again and nearly came to grief. Mr. Penrose managed to catch her flailing arm without dropping the sack he carried in his other hand.

"Careful, child, or your mama will have scolds to fire off for the next five years, and they will be justified." He spoke lightly, but not lightly enough.

"I was happy to see you," Holly said, a slight mulish angle coming into her jaw. "We don't want to call on Mrs. Colchester, but she owes Mama money for the sampler."

"Hollister Ann," Hope said, heat creeping up her neck. "One does not bruit one's business about in the street."

Holly looked from one adult to the other. "What's 'bruit'?"

"Bruit means," Mr. Penrose said, "to bray and roar and have no care for privacy or discretion. I passed a chorus of girls bruiting their holiday glee to the skies."

Holly repeated the word silently.

"You are delivering the completed sampler?" Mr. Penrose asked.

"We are. You've been shopping." And he'd been on the way to the house with his treasures. Hope was unaccountably, embarrassingly glad, which would not do at all.

"Noon has come and gone, and I've not yet had my midday meal. Why don't you ladies take the food home with you, and I will deliver the sampler? How much does Mrs. Colchester owe you?"

Hope named an embarrassingly small sum. "But you cannot deliver this to her like some ticket porter. She will be full of questions and draw all the wrong conclusions."

Mr. Penrose plucked the sampler from Hope's hands and passed her the sack, which was blessedly heavy.

"If she wants to pepper me with questions, she will have to order another sampler. I am merely making a delivery to ensure the customer has the goods by the agreed-upon date. The snow is picking up again. I'll see you back at the house."

He bounded up the steps with enviable energy. Hope considered telling him that if he meant to impersonate a ticket porter, he'd do so more effectively at the back door, but no kitchen maid would have payment on hand, and neither would the cook or housekeeper.

Not in Mrs. Colchester's demesne. The front door was the portal to payment from the butler or—Mrs. Colchester would be curious about the fellow delivering the finished work—the lady of the house herself.

"Come on, Mama, or we might lose our way in a terrible storm."

"You would vanquish the elements themselves, Hollister Ann."

Holly took Hope's free hand. "Papa used to talk to me like that. 'Here there be dragons!' There are no dragons, though."

Oh, but there were, unfortunately. And there were terrible, sudden storms, and as Mr. Penrose doffed his hat and was admitted to the Colchester abode, Hope had the sense just such a tempest was bearing down directly upon her.

CHAPTER FOUR

One of the first things Joshua had noticed about Quinn Wentworth was that he'd known exactly how to deal with widows. He was the soul of decorum with them, always patient, always able to grasp what the black-clad customer had only genteelly implied. The bereaved ladies had left the quiet opulence of his office feeling respected for stating reasonable needs.

With the families of those same widows, who viewed the lady as greedy, witless, doughty, or worse, simply for requesting access to her own funds, Quinn was the avenging angel of slighted duty.

The grasping, negligent, deceitful, or indifferent sons and daughters, even the nephews, brothers, or uncles, endured such a frigid, succinct scolding that they mended their ways and took their paws off the widow's mite they had no right to control.

Or the widower's mite, in a few notable cases.

Joshua was certain Quinn would have dealt thus even on Mrs. Colchester's behalf, though she was clearly prospering in her bereavement.

Maureen had given Joshua a whole different perspective on a widow's situation, on the sense of being cast into the role of the unvalued, lonely, sad, and bewildered relict. Americans did not go in for the most elaborate mourning rituals, but they did expect a widow to *retire* and live on psalms and sadness for a year or two.

"Your payment," Joshua said, putting two coins on the table before Hope. He'd come down the kitchen steps and found the ladies tying green candles into bundles with measured lengths of red ribbon.

"I need your finger," Holly said. "Right on the X."

Joshua obliged.

"This is twice the price Mrs. Colchester and I discussed," Hope said, staring at the coins. "I will take half back."

"You will do no such thing. She ordered another sampler—Let There Be Light. Same style and colors as the first. I suggested that procuring the supplies to make such a creation would be possible amid the holiday rush only if an advance was paid on the project. Your samplers are much in demand, and if Mrs. Colchester expects hers by Twelfth Night, she must reckon with the competition for your services."

Hope rose and put the coins in a tin on the mantel. The cat roused himself enough to watch her deposit her wages in her makeshift safe, then went back to dozing on the hearth.

"Thank you," she said. "Thank you most sincerely. Give me your coat. The hems are damp, and... Where is your scarf, Mr. Penrose?"

"Lost it." One of Gabriel's minions had needed it. "What's for lunch?"

"Food," Holly said, gathering up four more green candles. "Wonderful, hot food."

Hope smiled in the way of parents who were both amused and vexed by their offspring. "I thought I'd make ham-and-cheese sandwiches and toast them."

"Until the cheese melts," Holly added. "The ham is luscious. Mama let me have a bite."

"She let that useless disgrace of a feline have a bite too," Joshua said, handing over his coat. "He is the most spoiled creature in all of England."

"His presence is sweet and cheering. Heifer might be an angel unawares." Holly made a beckoning wave of her wrist, and Joshua again surrendered an index finger in the interests of tying a tidy bow.

"Last one! May I hang more snowflakes, Mama?"

"One dozen more, then you get yourself back here, Hollister Ann. You still have sums to do."

The girl took a dozen pieces of newsprint cutwork from a stack on the mantel, gathered up her cloak, and whisked up the kitchen steps.

"Where is she off to?"

"The conservatory." Hope unwrapped the loaf of bread, sniffed it, and closed her eyes. "She is decorating for the hens in hopes that cheerful biddies lay more eggs. How did you explain yourself to Mrs. Colchester?"

Hope got to work with a bread knife. Joshua washed his hands at the sink and looked about for something useful to do.

"She did not recognize me. I know her from before her husband went to his eternal reward, and she did not recognize me. She's near-sighted, which is a metaphor of some sort."

"The cheese slicer is above the tea drawer," Hope said. "My late husband's invention."

Joshua located what looked to be a device for lifting pieces of pie, except that the thing had a slit near the wide end that opened at a sharp angle. "How does one...?"

"Draw it toward you across the top of the cheese." Hope demonstrated, scraping a perfect, thin slice of cheese from the fat wedge Joshua had bought earlier.

Hope smelled of the balsam that must scent the candles, and when she stood close to Joshua, he realized she wasn't as tall as he'd thought. Slippers rather than heeled boots and proximity had her coming up only to his shoulder.

"Clever," Joshua said, giving the device a try as Hope went back to cutting bread. "I've seen wire used to scrape cheeses, but this creates a uniform thickness in the slice."

"Edwin patented it. He patented any number of inventions, but they never seem to come to anything. We do have some mustard, though it's quite vinegary."

Joshua would not take her last teaspoon of mustard. "Plain will do for me. Shipboard fare takes a toll on the digestion."

"You truly did arrive only last evening?"

"From New York. Everything everybody warned me about a winter crossing is true, though the food keeps better in the cold. I told Mrs. Colchester I am your lodger."

Hope stopped slicing. "You told her what?"

The question was quiet, but the inflection portended Significant Female Upset. Any man married for three days knew that tone, and Joshua had been married for eight hundred and twenty-five days. He had been grieving for what felt like an eternity.

"I told her I am your lodger. You have plenty of space. The neighborhood isn't that fancy, and widows do take in lodgers. Lodgers of the male variety are useful for shoveling coal and snow, we can open stuck flues, and we are very appreciative of even humble cooking."

"My lodger." Inchoate upset sounded as if it had deflated to consternation. "One must *do* for lodgers. Feed them, tend to their washing. I have considered lodgers—women only—but Mr. Peters advised against it."

"Who is Mr. Peters?" And why would he advise against a scheme that might put Hope on less perilous financial footing?

Hope rewrapped the loaf and put it in the breadbox at the end of the counter nearest the window.

"He is my solicitor. He was Edwin's solicitor, and he has been kind enough to look after my situation. He will handle the sale of this house, and he has been quite clear that a furnished dwelling, and a furnished family home rather than a lodging house or rental property, will bring the best price."

Joshua fetched the ham out of the window box, took up a meat knife, and began slicing. Not too thin, not too thick.

Shoveling snow had given him time to consider, or reconsider, the situation in his home. His evidence against Hope Burdette was insufficient to convict her of confidence tricks, and more to the point, he did not want to convict her.

"I have tried to convince myself that you are a swindler," he said. "You might well be trying to convince yourself of the same about me." He passed Hope the first slice.

She looked at the offering, accepted it, and took a nibble. "I have. You show up out of nowhere, in weather calculated to gain you admittance, and claim to own the house I've lived in for more than two years. You do bear a resemblance to the old fellow whose portrait is hanging in the foyer, but that could well be coincidence."

That she was also weighing evidence rather than making accusations came as an inordinate relief.

"I come home from years overseas," Joshua said, sawing gently, "and find my house, my home, the refuge I have looked forward to returning to, occupied by some woman of limited means and her daughter. They've been dwelling in my house rent-free for some time, if I can believe the woman." He took a small slice for himself. "I want to believe you, but I also know I own this place. Paid cash for it."

Hope popped the last of her ham into her mouth. "I want to believe you are some merchant returned from far-flung travels, but I know Edwin put every groat we had into buying this house, and I do pay a mortgage, Mr. Penrose. A substantial mortgage. Mr. Peters handles that as well, though the record does admit of some arrearages lately."

"Joshua, if I'm to be your lodger. Why not sell the art? It's worth quite a bit."

She snitched another bite of ham. "I did sell one piece—the oil of that big golden country house—and Mr. Peters was unhappy with me when he learned of it. He claimed the fading of the wallpaper gives away the missing art—he's right—and that people draw all the worst conclusions about a house with art ghosts in the wallpaper. I hung a sketch of Holly in place of the landscape—more of a house-scape, really—and haven't sold anything else."

"Chatsworth. Not my favorite. I am less fond of the seascapes than I used to be too. You have my permission to sell those, and we'll split the proceeds."

"You sell them," Hope replied, grinning. "You have a knack for a bargain. Why are we splitting the proceeds of sale?"

"Because you have maintained this property in salable condition without recompense for more than two years. Do you know what happens to abandoned buildings in London, Mrs. Burdette? They are soon occupied by thieves, rats, and beggars. Then the creeping damp starts, and there's no saving the place."

She eyed the pile of sliced ham, and Joshua could feel her hunger wrestling with her inherent self-restraint. He passed her a slice of cheese.

"How do you know about abandoned buildings?" she asked, munching the cheese and taking down from the crossbeam some sort of wire tray device with a long handle.

"I have bought and sold plenty of real estate." Joshua helped himself to a bite of cheese as well. "My grandfather had this house built, my late uncle lost it, and I bought it from his creditors. London is growing too fast, and solid structures are not as plentiful as they ought to be. This is some sort of toasting rack?"

"Exactly. The best toasting rack ever devised. It lets you cook four pieces at once rather than one at a time on the end of a fork. Edwin swore this would make us rich. Works best over a bed of coals."

She fashioned sandwiches of meat and cheese, arranged them just so between the racks of wire, and handed the lot to Joshua.

"I will make the tea and slice the apples," she said. "Mind you don't burn so much as a corner. Holly will not touch burned toast."

Joshua grasped, as he hadn't for a long time, the need to take care with what amounted to a meal for three. They had a bit of coin left-over from the shoveling money, and Hope's sampler had added to that meager store, but other than that...

Joshua scraped coals to one side in the big hearth and started toasting the sandwiches. He could take himself to the bank—half the metropolis away—and demand any amount of coin.

Why not do that?

"You are staring at the toast as if it holds all the secrets of eternal life." Hope tossed an apple core into a bucket and passed Joshua one-quarter of an apple.

"I have friends here in London. I could stay with them." The first side was browning nicely.

"You don't want to stay with them?"

Quinn and Jane were wonderful, lovely people and true friends. "They are besotted. Been married for years, and still... His letters sang panegyrics about her and conversely. I used to not mind it. I thought it foolish." And a bit annoying.

More than a bit.

"Mind the toast."

Joshua flipped the rack to start on the second side. What was he going on about?

"I do have lodgers, you know," Hope said, measuring a scoop of tea into a little sieve-like device. "Gabriel and his crew sometimes bide in the conservatory at night. The kitchen hearth goes right up through the conservatory—the bricks are exposed on the conservatory level—and that keeps the surrounds on the inside wall of the conservatory above freezing even if there's no fire in the conservatory hearth itself."

"Grandpapa's design. A conservatory in Town was an extravagance, but he made it a useful extravagance. Those boys have nowhere else to go?"

"Nowhere safe would be my guess. I hear them talking sometimes, and the sound is a comfort."

The sandwiches were golden on both sides, and Hope had sliced one and a half apples into twelve portions fashioned in a circle.

She was arranging mugs on a tea tray—not the fussy little cups they'd used before—and Joshua felt a pang for the departed Edwin Burdette. He was missing this. Missing the domestic chat that every couple casually enjoyed. Missing the way Hope's brows knit when she was working on a mental puzzle. Missing how she deftly parented a lively, intelligent, energetic daughter.

"I met my late wife when I sought to take a room in her lodging house," Joshua said, apropos of exactly nothing. "She lectured me sternly about muddy boots and being late to meals, and by the time she was warning me about watching my language in front of her son, I knew I wanted to propose."

Hope cut each sandwich into quarters, making a mess of crumbs on the counter. These she collected in her palm and also dumped into the bucket.

"Edwin swept me off my feet too. I wanted nothing in life so much as I wanted to become Mrs. Edwin Burdette. My family wouldn't hear of it."

"And yet, here you are, Mrs. Edwin Burdette, mother to Hollister Ann Burdette." Joshua rose, wondering what the conversation had accomplished. A cease-fire perhaps. An agreement to disagree. "What do you want most in life now?"

Hope put the sandwiches into an artful stack and brought the plate to the table. "Lunch, I suppose, but if I'm to be your landlady, you may, when we are not in public, address me as Hope."

Joshua put away the ham and cheese while Mrs. Burdette—Hope—saw to the tea tray. She bellowed up the steps for her daughter, and when Joshua did partake of his meal, he declared them the best sandwiches he'd ever eaten anywhere in his whole life.

And he was not exaggerating even a little.

CHAPTER FIVE

"One other item." Justinian Bartholomew Peters—J. Bartholomew in correspondence and to his colleagues, as distinguished from his late grandfather, Phineas Bartholomew Peters—adjusted the angle of his top hat. "Best send a basket around to our Mrs. Burdette. Poor thing was looking a bit peaky last time I saw her. Deduct the cost from her account, of course, and use your judgment regarding the lavishness of the contents. A bit of meat and cheese, some jams, jellies, and whatnot. A few sweet buns for the little girl. You're an enterprising fellow, Plodgely. I trust you implicitly."

Herman Plodgely was a hardworking fellow. J. Bartholomew would never have kept him on as the office's junior solicitor otherwise. Plodgely was also the sole support of his helpmeet of the past ten years and of three little Plodgelys. A fourth might be in the offing. Herman was looking worried and fatigued, the same expression that had accompanied Mrs. Plodgely's previous confinements.

"A basket for the widow. Of course, Mr. Peters. Tastefully ample rather than extravagant..." Plodgely glanced out the latticed window to the snow, which was becoming more ample by the hour. "Will we be selling Mrs. Burdette's house any time soon? I ask because prospective buyers might inquire during your absence, and one wants to be accurate with one's information."

"Then you accurately tell them that nobody buys or sells houses at Yuletide. Mrs. Burdette has made the decision to sell, but the timing has yet to be settled. One does not hurry a widow from the commodious surrounds of her formerly happy marital home."

Plodgely had the sort of open, cheerful countenance that inspired trust. He was blond, fair-skinned, solidly built, and plodding rather than brilliant. J. Bartholomew paid him well enough that nobody would steal him away, but not so well that Plodgely would grow complacent.

"But you said..." Plodgely had an excellent memory, sometimes annoyingly so.

"I said that when Mrs. Burdette had finished second mourning, the timing might be right to liquidate her real property. I realize that Mr. Burdette went to his reward more than two years ago, but honestly, Plodgely, would you and the missus want to look for accommodations at this time of year?"

A touching notion if one was telling biblical tales, but the deepening snow rather diminished the appeal of the reality.

"Of course you are right, sir, but Mrs. Plodgely and I do not enjoy the comfortable circumstances... That is to say, we are still building toward a secure future. Mrs. Burdette's spouse left her well provided for."

Mrs. Burdette's spouse had had a better mind for mechanical matters than any six geniuses combined. Fortunately, dear Edwin had also had no head for business.

J. Bartholomew wrapped his scarf about his neck. Black lamb's-wool was warm, practical, and soft. Perhaps next year, J. Bartholomew would treat himself to an angora scarf. Instant prosperity attracted notice, but a gradual rise in fortunes was almost to be expected for a competent man of business.

"Mrs. Burdette is not as well provided for as you might think, Plodgely. The house is quite nice, and the patent income is making good progress against the mortgage, but the mortgage remains substantial. That pesky matter of interest will rear its ugly head."

"If you say so, sir."

"I do say so." Gloves next. Black kid lined with rabbit fur. "Have you plans for the holidays, Plodgely?"

"Just the usual, sir. Goose with all the trimmings, plum pudding, snapdragon, a few tokens. My brother's family will join us. Missus does love the holidays."

And Plodgely loved his missus. All very sweet and exceedingly dull. "Give your missus my holiday felicitations, and here..." J. Bartholomew fished in his greatcoat pocket. "A penny each for the little ones from old Mr. Peters, eh?" He set the coins on the edge of Plodgely's desk. If one looked the part of Father Christmas—and Peters did—one should enjoy playing the role in minor ways. "Will that boy of yours be old enough to clerk for us soon?"

"Not for a few years, sir. Missus is powerfully in favor of book-learning until a lad turns twelve."

And Missus ruled the roost, of course. J. Bartholomew kept a wary distance from her. She was protective of her husband, which was understandable, but she was also exactly the sort to notice that J. Bartholomew always had reasons why now was not the time to sell the Burdette house.

The time would come, of course. No banker born and bred on English soil dithered about in the colonies indefinitely. Joshua Penrose's convenient absence would end, and he would return to a house waiting for him in more or less the same condition he'd left it.

Fortunately, Penrose was inured to wealth and comfort and no longer in the first blush of young manhood. He'd not willingly make a winter passage across the North Atlantic.

J. Bartholomew collected his brass-handled walking stick. "You're certain you don't mind tending the shop on your own over the holidays?" A silver handle would do for next year.

"The clerks will be in, and we'll muddle along well enough."

They'd while away the days playing whist and cribbage and

making the place smell of meat pies. Let them enjoy their petty pleasures for a few chilly days. By next year, the lot of them might well be out of work, while J. Bartholomew himself would be enjoying a secure retirement, thanks mostly to dear Edwin.

"Send word if anything urgent should arise." J. Bartholomew moved toward the door. "Open late, close early, but do maintain a presence. If we're too much in evidence over the holidays, the other solicitors will conclude we're desperate for business. If we're absent without leave, they'll conclude we have no business at all."

"I have plenty to do, sir, what with the year-end accountings. You enjoy a well-earned respite."

Such a trusting soul. J. Bartholomew departed amid a chorus of happy-Christmas-and-to-you-toos from the clerks, and as he made his way down the snowy street, he reflected that it truly was a happy Christmas.

Because of a lot of foolish gadgets, J. Bartholomew was becoming not merely comfortable, but well-off. He would dispense a small portion of that good fortune to Burdette's widow and explain that the mortgage had taken the lion's share of the patent earnings.

Of course, there was no mortgage. Burdette had believed himself to be the sole owner of the property in fee simple absolute, paying the total price in cash. The inspiration to invent a mortgage when explaining Burdette's finances to the grieving widow had been nothing short of genius.

There was no mortgage, there had been no purchase of the property. The cash Burdette had parted with was real enough and generating interest in the cent-per-cents. The income from the little gadgets was equally real. Such a pity that Joshua Penrose's ownership of the house also fell under the heading of an undeniable reality.

J. Bartholomew resolved to extricate Mrs. Burdette from Mr. Penrose's house soon.

Soon. Not yet, but soon.

He tossed a copper to the crossing sweeper shivering by his

meager barrow of horse droppings. The coin landed in the snow, and the lad fell to his knees to search for his buried treasure.

"Happy Christmas," J. Bartholomew called.

The boy's reply was inaudible. J. Bartholomew went along home to a spiced toddy and a roaring fire, before which he indulged in one of his favorite hobbies—sketching the villa in the South of France where he would enjoy a contented and well-funded old age.

~

"Henceforth," Hope said, smoothing Holly's hair back from her brow, "until I am an old granny, I will have to do the storybook voices because of you, Joshua Penrose."

And he'd done them so well, adopting a mincing falsetto for the grandmama and a growling baritone for the wolf. His young lady had sounded cultured and intelligent, and his woodsman had been manly virtue made audible.

Joshua rose from the rocking chair. "At one of my places of employment, we hired boys off the street to do the work of taking messages, delivering documents, and so forth. They were housed at the business, and in an effort to encourage them toward literacy, somebody had the idea to start reading them stories. One developed some thespian skills of necessity. Our boys were a demanding audience."

Hope was certain that Joshua had had that idea, or he'd certainly championed it. "Did they learn to read?"

"They did, and then we took a notion of assigning each new boy an older fellow to mentor and instruct him. The literacy problem solved itself in less than two years."

Something about the solved problem bothered him. "You liked reading those stories."

He held out his hand. "I did. I believe you mentioned a bite of shortbread as a reward for good behavior?"

For the first time in ages, Hope allowed a man to assist her to rise.

"A small less-than-fresh bite. I'm saving most of it for Holly." Who had struggled mightily to keep her eyes open for the duration of the story, then fallen instantly to sleep.

"You should save it all for her. She is an exceedingly well-behaved child." Joshua stretched luxuriously and tugged the covers up around Holly's shoulders."

The gesture was natural and protective and not one Hope had ever seen Edwin make.

"Remind me," Joshua went on, "to avoid the near occasion of shoveling snow. I went to seed on board ship, and wielding a shovel takes muscle."

Hope preceded him into the kitchen, leaving the door to the housekeeper's bedroom open for warmth. She'd long ago rearranged those quarters so the bed occupied the front room, where the parlor stove was to be found, and any furniture intended for the sitting room occupied the colder, disused back chamber.

"I do have a bit of the poppy somewhere in the larder if you're in pain," Hope said.

"Thank you, but no. To exert myself felt good at the time. What shall we do about this house, Hope?"

To be Hope to an adult male, not Mrs. Burdette or Widow Burdette, required an adjustment, a small step away from being defined by bereavement and lack rather than by one's own identity.

Edwin would have told her that it was past time to take those steps. "We shall be grateful for shelter of any kind, given the present weather." Hope was dodging a significant issue, but she truly did not want to turn Joshua out with no place to go. "Will peppermint tea do?"

"Splendidly. I have a proposal regarding this dwelling."

Hope swung the kettle over the coals, fished out two peppermint sachets from the tin holding her store, and took down the two best mugs.

"I might have to consult with my solicitor regarding any proposals. Mr. Peters has been a font of knowledge and good judgment so far. I do believe that when my mortgage payments are late, he makes the payment on time for me and lets me catch up without demanding any interest. I know the bank expects interest and fees and whatnot."

Joshua set the sugar bowl on the table. "This is a valuable property in a good neighborhood. Whatever the extent of the mortgage, the property has appreciated substantially since Edwin purchased it —if he purchased it."

"Which he did. I raised that topic of the house's value with Mr. Peters, and he said the press wants everybody to think London is prospering, that Town is growing by leaps and bounds, and the streets are paved with gold. He claims the reality is different. That few people have enough coin to afford a place like this, and I should not expect to make a great deal on the sale."

But she would make something. He'd assured her of that.

"More and more families have enough coin to purchase a nice house, Hope. Many prospered during the war and learned to do it without relying on agriculture for their income. The Corn Laws will keep the gentry flush for a while, and they are always shopping for Town properties."

Before the kettle could whistle in earnest and wake Holly, Hope took it off the fire and poured two steaming mugs. The aroma of peppermint filled the kitchen, a reminder that in warmer seasons, the back garden did more than look pretty.

"Every time I ask Mr. Peters if the market is right to sell this house, he has a reason not to let it go yet. I think he fears Holly and I will be homeless, which..."

Joshua took both mugs to the table. "Which...?"

"Isn't likely, but I don't see that we can afford to live here much longer. I have family in the shires who would probably look after Holly if I begged them to." Probably, assuming they still lived at the last address Hope had for them. "What is your proposal?"

She joined Joshua at the table as the cat departed from his place on the hearth and strode across the corridor into the darkened bedroom. He'd climb on the bed and snuggle up to Holly, and she'd sleep a little more warmly for his presence.

"You worry about that lazy beast," Joshua said, putting a lump of sugar into each mug. "I do believe Mrs. Colchester might take him in."

Holly worried about Heifer, and thus Hope worried for him doubly. "Mrs. Colchester would not be caught dead with a creature of such low repute in her pantry."

"He's handsome, dignified, and behaves himself. Doesn't claw the curtains, never messes in the house, repels mice with his mere presence. If you asked her, one widow to another, she'd aid you, and you'd be doing her a favor as well. I suspect she's quite lonely."

Hope sipped the tea, savoring both the sweetness and the bracing aroma of peppermint. "You might be right. How do you know such things?"

"I have been in trade for years, in the financial end of trade. People make a choice about how they react to hardship and lack. Some rise to the challenge, sharing what little they have, sparing a kind word if they can't spare anything more. Others are diminished by their straitened circumstances. Still others are diminished by improved circumstances. Their good fortune provokes in them such a fear of losing what they have that they become worse misers than they ever were when poor."

"I am not poor. Edwin used to say that a lack of coin did not make one poor. A lack of imagination and the freedom to use it were the worse deprivations."

"And yet," Joshua said, gaze on the dwindling pile of lumps in the sugar bowl, "Edwin's daughter and his cat and his widow must eat. Are you ever angry with him?"

Not a question Hope had been asked before. "Furious, from time to time. Any number of people told me I was married to a genius, but the genius could not keep a ledger to save himself, nor would he allow me to do the requisite bookkeeping."

Hope told herself to stop there, then told herself that Joshua could be trusted with the truth.

"Edwin was the most playful, endearing papa a girl ever had, but if Holly had been naughty, that was always for me to deal with even if dear Papa had instigated the bad behavior. He would go for walks, be gone for hours in all weather, and tell me that he needed to move to think sometimes. In truth, he needed to get away from a colicky baby or a wife who had a megrim coming on. He'd be over at the Ocelot telling stories by the hour."

"And then," Joshua said, "he'd shut himself in a room and beg to be allowed to sit for hours, because he needed solitude and a comfortable chair to think at other times. My wife was a fanatic about dust. Maureen kept all the chairs and sofas in the public rooms covered nearly all the time. What is the sense in having pretty furniture if it must be shrouded in Holland covers six days a week?"

True male bewilderment colored Joshua's question.

"But somehow," Hope said, "you grasped that dust was an enemy she could subdue, so you did not begrudge her her victories. Does it feel disloyal to criticize her?"

Joshua peered at his tea. "Not as disloyal as it once did. I loved her, and I cherish her memory, but she was human, as I was, and am. I think it's a mistake to glorify a past that was precious and lovely, but imperfect. Maureen warned me not to climb into the grave with her. She was very brave, very principled."

And fierce, apparently, at least where dust and a beloved husband were concerned. "She sounds well worth missing."

"As does your Edwin. Maureen also admonished me not to put her memory on any pedestals. How did we get on this subject?"

"The cat, Mrs. Colchester, Edwin's ghost making me angry. You are avoiding this proposal you've mentioned about the house."

And Hope had allowed Joshua to meander away from the topic. She did not want to charge him rent—they'd eaten today and would eat for several more days because of his ingenuity and hard work—

but she also did not want him getting too comfortable at a residence he had no right to occupy.

And yet, to have a conversation that was neither hurried nor particularly pragmatic was a rare luxury, to have a confidant more precious still, and Hope frankly did not care what Edwin's ghost had to say regarding either topic.

"I left England in something of a hurry," Joshua said, setting down his mug. "My business partner had recently married, much was in flux, and my decision to travel had about it a now-or-never quality."

Like Hope's decision to marry Edwin, oddly enough. She'd been so anxious that some clever idea would seize his attention, and all thoughts of courtship and matrimony would fly from his head.

"Did your business partner marry well?" she asked.

Joshua's lips quirked. "Very well, better than he knew, and the extent of his good fortune was becoming more apparent to him by the day—and night. Quinn and Jane were fashioned for each other by providence itself. If anything, marriage made his head for business more astute when he was nigh unparalleled in his expertise to begin with. A fanatic for financial dealings."

"You are not a fanatic?" And what did a profession in *financial dealings* involve, anyway? Wentworth and Penrose was a London bank, but Joshua could hardly be associated with that institution when he'd been overseas for years.

"I am not a fanatic, and it's probably more accurate to say that Quinn is an artist. I am a dedicated appreciator of the financial arts and competent as a result. A large part of my job was managing Quinn, and once Jane got her mitts on him, I was surplus to requirements."

He finished his tea and set his mug aside, his expression puzzled.

"Are you figuring this out only now?" How much of Hope's job had been managing Edwin? How much did she miss that job, and how much did she miss the merry, impecunious, often-distracted man she'd married?

"I am figuring out my motives from a new perspective," Joshua said. "I see now that I haven't wanted to intrude on their happiness. I also haven't wanted their happiness to intrude on my sorrow."

"Ah. Widows have a different challenge. We are stashed away with little but our grief to keep us company for at least a year, and for that whole time, we're spared any semblance of functioning, at least in theory. Among the lower orders, where I now number, the theory is quite useless. I imagine your Maureen hadn't the luxury of moping about for years. Men, by contrast, are given almost no time to grieve. Both approaches strike me as disrespectful to the person suffering the loss."

"Disrespectful. Good word. Unfeeling, and indicative of a society trying to elude its own mortality. More hot water?"

"No, thank you. Tell me what you have in mind for the house?"

"Before we come to any final arrangement, you should consult Mr. Peters, and I will review what documents my solicitors have regarding the property. For the present, I propose that we allow the whole matter to wait until after the New Year. That's less than a fortnight, and that fortnight, according to every earthly authority, is supposed to be merry and bright. I am newly returned from years of travel. I need to get my bearings, and for that matter, I don't even have my luggage yet."

"You propose that we do nothing?" The notion had so much seductive appeal, Hope was instantly skeptical of it. "We simply rub along, boarder and landlady, for the duration of the holidays?"

"Yes, more or less. I have proven that I can be useful to the household. Counsel for the defense points to my expert shoveling skills and my unique ability to impersonate both a wolf and a convincing granny. More to the point, something as significant as the sale of a house or the creation of a mortgage on a house is always well documented. Your Mr. Peters, the bank, somebody has information we both need to resolve ownership of the house."

"This is *my house*, Joshua Penrose. My husband paid dearly for it. Too dearly for me to cede the field without a fight."

He saluted with his empty mug. "This is *my house*, Hope Burdette. I paid dearly to retrieve it from creditors who would have demolished a fine old building to put up cheap tenements where my legacy stood. Then I paid yet more to bring this place back up to the standards my grandfather set for it. I will not cede the field without a good reason for doing so."

Hope finished her tea, which had cooled to lukewarm. "You admit that such a reason might exist?"

"I don't want to."

"I am determined to go down fighting, if defeat is to be mine. But..." Edwin had been an utter dunderhead where money was concerned and too prideful to allow Hope to manage anything more than her pin money.

"But Edwin could be rackety." Joshua rose and put the sugar bowl back in the breadbox. "He might have signed a lease-to-own agreement, which has been voided by your late mortgage payments. We simply don't know. I grew a bit rackety myself." He resumed his seat just as one of the candles on the mantel guttered.

Rackety. Hope and rackety were familiar foes. She did not like the sound of that lease-to-own business at all, and it hadn't occurred to her that a few late payments might open the door to foreclosure.

The notion of Joshua describing himself as rackety, though... She patted his hand. "Were you forgetful at times? Weepy for no reason? You couldn't sleep through the night, but then you'd drag yourself through the day in a fog? When you finally started feeling a bit more like yourself, everybody treated you as if you were the barmy old auntie who came to supper in her riding habit?"

Joshua caught her fingers, gave them a squeeze, and let go. "The uncle who wore his shooting jacket to Sunday services. I tried to be mindful of my business affairs, but I must admit that some document or other might have had less than my full attention. The possibility is remote, but Eric went to his reward, and that... I was not expecting to ever weather that blow."

The weathering, based on Joshua's expression, was ongoing. "Eric?"

"My step-son. He preceded his mother in death by twenty-four hours. I never told her he was gone, but I think she knew."

Of course she'd known, but she'd allowed her husband to spare her the news because that was one of few gifts he could give his fading wife.

"She loved you very much, Joshua, and you loved her and that boy."

"He was easy to love. They both were." Said simply, a recitation of facts holding back an ocean of sentiment. "One day, Maureen was whistling Christmas carols—she was a virtuosic whistler, despite the horrid impropriety of the habit for ladies—and the next, she'd developed a slight cough. By the time she took to her bed, Eric had a slight cough too. More than slight. I don't remember much of the ensuing fortnight, but I remember her lectures."

What a hammering fate had delivered to his heart. A cruel disruption of not only life, but of faith in the natural order.

Children were not to precede their parents in death. To think otherwise was to contemplate an unspeakable offense to the heart.

"You remember the love," Hope said. "The love makes the loss both worse and bearable." What had any of this to do with deeds and mortgages and solicitors? Nothing and everything. "I accept your proposal. We will agree to disagree regarding ownership of this house, for now. When the New Year comes, we'll see what's to be done."

"Because you feel sorry for me? I did not tell you of my loss to elicit pity, Hope."

His losses. Plural. Another candle guttered. "When Edwin died, all I could think was that Holly would be next. I'd have to go back to my family, whom I haven't heard from in years. No note of condolence, no little card at the holidays. Then I was caught up with the notion that I might die, and Holly would be consigned to the poorhouse. Had Mr. Peters not kept matters sorted for me, I'm sure I could have unwittingly signed away this house. You do not have my pity, Joshua. You have my understanding."

He sat back. "I'll take it and be grateful." His relief was evident in the first true smile Hope had seen from him. "I am your lodger until the New Year. You are my landlady. I propose that, by way of rent, you make me responsible for stocking the larder, and if I can manage a few sacks of coal, I'll do that as well."

Inordinate, unreasonable relief cascaded through Hope, along with a touch of hesitance. With nothing more than a shovel and some ingenuity, Joshua had provided immediate rations for Hope, Holly, and the lot of ragged boys.

If something—or someone—seemed too good to be true... And yet, there was no more good silver left to steal, and the coalhole was nearly empty.

"Shall I make you up a bedroom? We have all the linens and such, and the main apartment is quite comfortable."

"I slept there for years, and I agree, but coal is dear, and we have little enough of it. Heating the kitchen and the study will tax us sufficiently that I'll make do with the sofa. When my luggage arrives, we can pawn some of the contents—I won't be needing my dancing slippers—and Holly will have her happy Christmas."

Ah. He was doing this in part for Holly. Hope respected him for that. "We have a bargain," she said, extending her hand across the table.

He shook, his smile becoming bashful. "Shall I bank the fire or wash the mugs?"

"You tend to the fire." Hope rose, fatigue hitting her as a physical heaviness in her limbs. Worry did that, weighted the whole body with doom.

She rinsed out the mugs, dumped the contents of the tea sachets into the hens' bucket, and resisted the urge to cry.

The holidays had become an ordeal since Edwin's passing, not that they'd been unfailingly jolly in previous years. To spend this Yuletide with companionship, with an ally even, was an unlooked-for boon. Whatever was true about ownership of the house, Joshua Penrose was a decent man, and he'd not see her and Holly turned out without a groat.

He blew out the remaining candles, which left only the banked coals to illuminate the kitchen.

Hope crossed to the hearth, wrapped him in a swift hug, and drew back. "Thank you. An agreement to disagree is eminently sensible. I'll see you in the morning."

He bowed slightly in the darkness. "Until morning."

Hope hurried off to her bedroom, half mortified by her own forwardness and half tempted to repeat it.

Which would not do. At all.

CHAPTER SIX

Breakfast had been more ham, cheese, and bread. Joshua was grateful to have had shelter for the night. Grateful for his health. Grateful to have made a safe passage across the Atlantic. Grateful, grateful, grateful, and grateful for the breakfast fare.

He was also tired of it. He was tired of puzzling out how to raise more cash when his trunks had apparently disappeared to the North Pole. He was tired of being cold and tired of being tired, and he had let himself in for two more weeks of this holiday joy.

What was I thinking?

He'd been thinking of how not to cast Hope and Holly on the charity of their negligent family. How to avoid being a holiday guest at the ducal residence. How to put off admitting that, in fact, he might have signed away Grandpapa's residence in a fog of grief and exhaustion.

And as to that, a wing chair and a hassock provided no better rest than did a lumpy, too-short sofa.

"Heifer is my friend," Holly said, dangling a string before the cat's nose. "I must give him a Christmas token because he gives me the gift of his friendship all year."

The cat took a halfhearted swipe at the string, then strode off across the conservatory's brick flooring to recline beneath a venerable camellia.

"You spoil him rotten, Hollister Ann, and as soon as you're asleep, he helps himself to the warmth you radiate."

"I know. I help myself to his warmth too. And he is wonderfully soft. What shall I get him for his token?"

The cat was wonderfully indolent. Joshua had forgotten how persistent children could be. How annoyingly persistent, bless the little dears.

"Give him a flower. The camellias are about at their peak." Thank goodness Grandpapa had had them planted on the warmer side of the conservatory. The biddies were also penned on that side, clucking softly as they scratched in the dirt.

"Mama likes flowers. Will you give her a token for Christmas?"

My ancestral home with all the trimmings. Joshua shoved the fading remains of a potted lemon aside. He was looking for another shovel, his own having been contributed to Gabriel's future enterprises. The conservatory had had its own supply of coal once upon a time, and where there was coal, one frequently found shovels.

"Will you give Mama a special little gift," Holly went on, "all wrapped up with paper and colored string?"

"I have known your mother but a handful of days, child. A Christmas token would be presumptuous." A proper token would necessitate cash, shopping, more shopping, a bit of ribbon, a note on pretty paper. The gesture was meant to sound simple—a small gift to symbolize warm feelings—but in actuality, the process done right could be complicated.

As any husband or dedicated suitor knew. Joshua had felt slightly resentful of the whole business, until he'd endured a Yuletide season with nobody to give a token to.

"I wish we could give Mama gingerbread. She loves warm gingerbread with melted butter."

Joshua was abruptly famished for warm gingerbread with melted butter. "Help me look for the shovel, Holly. The shovel is how we might be able to purchase gingerbread and butter."

"Mrs. Colquitt pays Mama in butter. Mama teaches their servants to read because the housekeeper hasn't the patience, but the Colquitts go to the country for Christmas. They get their butter from the country, and so they have lots and lots of it."

Another potted lemon was summarily pushed closer to the window. "How jolly for them."

"Will you give me a holiday token?" Holly asked, joining her cat by the camellias.

No, I will not... Joshua abruptly stopped heaving trees about. *Decisions have consequences, many of them unintended.*

The voice in his head belonged to Quinn Wentworth. His Grace of Walden, rather. Quinn could think a question into tiny, unrecognizable pieces, while Joshua had excelled at seeing the good that might come of each potential choice.

Deciding to offer Hope a truce had held up to scrutiny from many angles, but Holly, with her persistent questions, presented Joshua with a consequence he'd not considered.

Children could grow quickly attached, to pets, to people, to places, even to toys or trees.

Their capacity for fondness was indiscriminate and passionate and could have sad, sad repercussions.

"Holly, I am but a temporary lodger here, for all we know. You might not see much of me past the end of the year." Putting the reality into words earned another tree—a sizable orange boasting a dozen unripened fruits—a swift trip across the conservatory.

"Are you going back to America?"

"No." Joshua had tried making life in America work, but without Maureen and Eric... Not a chance.

"It would not matter if you did." Holly stroked her cat's head, and the conservatory filled with stentorian purring. "You and I are friends. We'd write letters, and you could send me a token, though it would take ever so long to arrive. I could send one to you too."

I am not your friend. And yet, Joshua would not soon forget Holly or her mother, or the sudden surge of longing that had gone through him when Hope had surprised him with a hug at bedtime.

Not lust. *Longing.*

"Holly, you give your friendship too easily. I might well steal away in the night, and you'd never see me again."

She picked up the cat and hugged him, and damned if the beast did not reciprocate by rubbing his head beneath the child's chin. Shameless fraud.

"You are my friend. You would not disappear like that, unless you had to go spy on Napoleon or something, but old Wellie beat Napoleon to smithereens at Waterloo."

Old Wellie's army had taken a fearful drubbing on the same occasion. "Where would you hide a shovel if you were trying to keep it safe during a long absence?"

"Shovels are big. A shovel would be hard to hide. You could bury it. The conservatory has bare ground near the glass well. The hens might be guarding the buried shovel treasure!"

Nobody would bury a shovel, for pity's sake. "Where else?" The conservatory was nowhere near as crowded as it would have been had Joshua been in residence. The camellias were putting on a worthy show, but the citrus trees were anemic, the palms were straggly, and the spices mostly dormant. The ferns by the window were in shabby condition and making a mess for six feet in every direction.

The scent was off, too, thanks to the hens. Earth and greenery, but with the pungent tang of resident fowl added to the mix.

A conservatory stuffed cheek by jowl with thriving plants would have stayed warmer. One free of hens would have been quieter and less aromatic.

"That bare ground once sported roses," Joshua said. Grandmama's pride and joy. "Let's look in the cupboards, shall we?" A workbench along one wall had been set up like a kitchen counter, with cupboards below and a sink with a rusty pump on the end nearest the hearth.

"Heifer says the mice like the cupboards because they are warm."

"Heifer ought to say the mice would never hide in the cupboards, because the fiercest predator in the jungle will come along and eat them."

One cupboard held two dozen small, entirely useless, matching vases. Another housed folded burlap sacks. Most were empty save for mouse droppings. All were musty and dusty.

Joshua closed the last cupboard with a bit of force, which earned him a scowl from the cat in Holly's arms.

Why not hike to the bank, announce himself returned from the ends of the earth, and impose upon Quinn and Jane's hospitality? Leave Hope and Holly in peace for the next two weeks, then arrange for them to rejoin Hope's family. Mother and child would be safe, and Joshua would be warm, well fed, and...

Miserable. Miserable in a way that eclipsed bad sleep and boring menus by miles. Jane and Quinn would spend their holidays lurking beneath mistletoe, Ned would whistle jaunty carols, and the girls... Quinn's sisters were not girls anymore. Had not been for some time. Even Cousin Duncan, the family expert in quiet good sense, had gone for a happily married husband, and to a duchess, no less.

"You should look in the coal closet," Holly said, rubbing her cheek against the cat's crown. "Gabriel says it's filthy. He's my friend too. He says I'm just a girl, but Mama has promised me that stating the obvious is what boys do when they haven't anything truly witty to offer."

"Coal closet." Joshua had assumed the conservatory coal storage had long since been emptied, but, well, yes. "Logical. Of course. If you did get me a holiday token, I would be delighted with a ripe, juicy orange."

"I love oranges."

"Lack of fresh fruit is making me stupid." He moved one of the lemon trees he'd already wrestled with and considered what appeared to be a door to the garden, except it wasn't. Grandpapa had built the coal shed onto the northern side of the conservatory. The structure was convenient to the alley, provided one had keys to the door in the garden wall on the exterior side, and out of sight of the street.

The hinges were rusty, of course—conservatories were notoriously good at collecting damp—but Joshua was in a foul enough mood that a few hearty shoves and muttered curses saw the door budging open a good foot.

"What are you two getting up to?" Hope closed the conservatory door with her hip, her hands being full of a dish covered with a towel.

"Mama has brought gifts from afar!" Holly set the cat aside and bounded across the conservatory. "Did you come from the east, Mama?"

"I came from the kitchen. Mrs. Colquitt's housekeeper stopped by, and she brought both butter and gingerbread. This will tide us over until lunch. Joshua, what are you peering at?"

Gingerbread would tide Joshua over for the next twenty minutes, but what he'd found in the coal closet would warm his heart and his toes for weeks.

"Ladies, I suspect you were both very good all year, because this coal shed is half full, and I see not one, but two shovels against the back wall."

"We have coal?" Hope came closer slowly, as if unwilling to believe even the evidence of her eyes.

"We have a big pile of coal," Holly said, "and we have gingerbread and butter and flowers. This is going to be the best Christmas ever!" She grabbed the trunk of the lemon tree and spun around it as if it were a maypole.

Coal, lots and lots of coal. Joshua had beheld larger piles of coal, but none so wonderful as the old mess in the coal closet before him now.

Hope slipped an arm around his waist and rested her head on his shoulder. "Stinky, filthy, costly coal. A treasure indeed. Perhaps you were a good fellow all year too."

Joshua had been a sad, dutiful fellow, but in that moment,

sadness and duty were nowhere to be found. He'd done something right in Hope's eyes, and the look she turned on him was the very best holiday token he could have asked for.

He kissed her cheek, a gesture of sheer rejoicing, and she beamed at him.

"Gingerbread with butter seems a fitting way to celebrate," Hope said, holding up the plate.

Joshua took a slice—not the thickest—and held it up to Hope's mouth. She nibbled, he nibbled, and they shared their slice while Holly bellowed about hark the harried angels singing, and Heifer curled up for a nap beneath the blooming camellias.

"Found him!" Ned's triumph was spoiled by a subsequent sneeze. He produced a handkerchief, sneezed again, and came up smiling. "Our Joshua has gone to ground in the most obvious, least likely place. His own house."

Quinn glanced at Jane, who was smiling as well, though his duchess was also clearly puzzled by Ned's good news.

Her needle went still, and she put her embroidery on top of her workbasket. "I thought he sold that house when he married? Or, no... after that. The place stood empty for a time, but then he must have sold it. A family was living there. Perhaps he only rented it out?"

Quinn set aside his ledger and took off his glasses. "Jane, have you been spying?"

A conspiratorial glance flicked between Jane and young Ned. They were as thick as thieves—thicker, in fact, according to Ned, who knew of what he spoke.

"Keeping an eye on matters for a friend," Jane said, rising from her wing chair. "Why hasn't Joshua sent us a message, Quinn?"

"He's hibernating," Ned said, sparing Quinn an answer. "Going back to his hidey-hole. He has a fine old house to put him in mind of all the good times before he went and banished himself. He's getting his land legs, and then we'll hear from him."

Ned was nobody's fool, though Quinn still wasn't sure how the boy he'd met in prison had grown so tall. When had Ned stopped dropping aitches, and how had he learned to dress like a perfect gentleman?

All very mysterious, though Jane had figured prominently in the metamorphosis. Most of the credit went to Ned himself, though. A more determined soul did not walk the earth.

"Why go to ground when we were expecting to host him for the holidays?" Jane asked, worrying a nail. "A house of any size takes days to heat and provision, and few people are in search of posts at a time of year when we all seek to be with family."

"Not all of us have family." Quinn rubbed the bridge of his nose. "Family worth acknowledging, that is." The Wentworths were a family largely because Jane had made them so. She had the tenacity and resourcefulness common to many a preacher's daughter and a largeness of heart that Quinn marveled at regularly.

Ned settled in a corner of the sofa and picked up Jane's discarded embroidery. "I see it like this," he said, freeing the needle from the fabric. "Joshua hasn't any family here in London. But he did have family in New York. We're his family, but we're not *that* family. Might be, he's getting his courage up. When he greets us again, he says a little bit of goodbye—another goodbye—to the family he left in America."

The family he'd *buried* in America. Quinn still had the letter. *Regret to relate that Maureen and young Eric were gathered to untimely rewards prior to Christmas. Influenza, then lung fever. A common progression. Your condolences are appreciated in anticipation. Penrose.*

The shortest, saddest, most alarming letter Quinn had ever received.

"I should write him a note," Jane said. "Welcome him home. Let him know we're missing him, but content to leave the timing of a reunion to him."

Ned minutely shook his head as he began a delicate line of green stitches on the white linen. His embroidery was technically the equal to Jane's and creatively superior to it for never having been subjected to the guiding hands of governesses or nannies.

"Ned says we need to exercise patience," Quinn observed. "I agree with him. Joshua promised a return by the New Year, and we assumed he'd be our guest. Our holiday invitation might have slipped his mind. He might be waiting for his luggage to be sorted. Nobody wants to present himself as a holiday caller in his dressing gown and Hessians."

Jane made a face that belied her lofty social status. "I hate being patient."

"But you do it so well," Quinn replied. "Witness, the gentlemen whose company you keep in this room, who were once a pair of ruffians."

Ned held up his handiwork, then resumed stitching. "I was an urchin, thank you very much. You were the ruffian. A ruffian banker. Now you are a ducal ruffian banker."

Ned and Quinn had both been lost, and Jane had found them. Every instinct Quinn possessed bellowed that Joshua was now lost. He'd not be found with the usual holiday feasting and diversions. He'd have to navigate his own way home, and when he did, Quinn and Jane would rejoice loudly indeed.

"I am due to meet with Vicar regarding altar flowers," Jane said, glancing at the clock. "That man can make shortbread and tea cakes disappear like some sort of street conjurer handed a shiny sovereign."

"Goes with the profession," Ned said. "Same with urchins and ruffian bankers. We adore our sweets. If Vicar brings up the choir again, you will inform him that I have lost my voice. I will not get it back until summer. His Grace has a fine bass, though."

"Mind your tongue, Ned." Once upon a time, that growl would have chastened Ned.

"I am an honest man," Ned retorted. "Our duchess is contemplating a bit of mendacity, though. Jane wants to tell Vicar she has a megrim while she slips out the kitchen door and makes a discreet pass, or three, by Joshua's house."

"Four," Jane said, "before I knock on the door and ask if anybody has seen any misplaced bankers fresh from New York."

"Smoke is coming from two chimneys," Ned said. "The kitchen and what I presume must be a bedroom, but not the largest apartment on the back corner of the second floor."

Jane's frown eased. "Smaller rooms are easier to heat."

"The front and back walkways are shoveled clean," Ned went on, "as is the whole street. I spotted footprints all over the back garden. Himself is cozy, and somebody is tending to his kitchen hearth. Other somebodies are bustling about the garden as servants do when passing between households. You need not fret that Joshua is shivering in his own garret."

Ned, who had endured his share of shivering in garrets, had doubtless done that reconnaissance for Jane's sake. Also for Quinn's.

"Thank you, Neddy." Jane kissed his cheek. "You have just condemned me to forty-five minutes of Vicar's ruminations on the symbolism of stars in the night sky, but then, Cook will make her anise biscuits in the shape of stars, won't she?"

"Speaking of biscuits...?" Ned turned on Jane his hopeful-little-lad look, which had at some point become his charming-young-fellow look.

"To blazes with you and that bottomless pit you call a tummy, Ned Wentworth. I am off to serve my penance with Vicar. You two reprobates can just go hungry until luncheon." Jane kissed Quinn's cheek and departed.

She and Vicar would do equal justice to the treats, and the symbolism of empty plates and full bellies would earn honorable mention in Vicar's maunderings. He and Jane were great good friends, though half the world seemed to enjoy that status where Jane was concerned. She was no sort of duchess, in the opinion of some.

Quinn adored Jane's brand of duchessing.

"What else?" he asked as Ned switched from green thread to blue.

"Something peculiar is afoot. The footprints in the garden are mostly too small to be adult, and there's a cat making free with the property as well. Go one or two streets over, and the walkways aren't nearly as clear. When I asked about that, I was told a gang of boys led by a gent in fine tailoring whipped through the whole job yesterday."

"Description of the gent?"

"Tall, well-spoken, blond, no gloves, no scarf, but a coat fine enough for Bond Street, despite boots that had seen better days."

"Nobody shovels snow in his newest pair from Hoby's. What do you make of it?"

Ned began on a line of fine blue stitches exactly paralleling the row of green he'd just finished. "Joshua's house has a conservatory, and rumor is that's one of the places a lot of street boys go for makeshift shelter, but the fact is, there's a widow and her little girl living in that house. The cat has house privileges as well."

Ned's gift for observation of details had been learned in a hard school from which Quinn had graduated as well. "Anything else?"

"Nobody has seen any trunks delivered to that address in the past day or two, but then, most of London is still shoveling out."

"Or waiting for a thaw to come along. Do you know if Joshua sold that property?" Quinn and his partner observed a scrupulous mutual lack of interest in each other's personal finances.

"You're the banker. I don't see how a widow who can afford to light only two fires in the whole house would acquire the place outright. Might be a private mortgage somewhere, or she could have inherited the property, but a bank mortgage is also a possibility."

By damn, Ned was a credit to his upbringing—all of his upbringing.

Quinn slipped his glasses into a breast pocket and rose. "You'll set a watch on the place?"

"Already done."

"I'm away lest Vicar accost me to play a shepherd in his Christmas pageant."

Ned's needle went still. "Shepherd. Spare me. Where are you off to?"

"The bank."

"I'll come with you." He tucked the needle into a corner of the fabric and got to his feet. "Of course, we'll miss the tray Jane ordered for us."

"We'll depart through the mews by way of the kitchen. I paraded about in my dressing gown with a towel on my head for the amusement of the faithful two years ago. One does not forget such an ordeal."

"And the lamb. You holding that squirming, bleating lamb and trying to look holy was the best part."

"I still have the dressing gown, Edward Wentworth, and Jane can take it in to fit you."

Ned made for the door. "Meet you by the pantries."

Quinn beat him by two minutes, or two biscuits, as holiday timekeeping went. All the way to the bank, Quinn considered who might be holding the mortgage on Joshua's former residence. He also wondered about the widow who'd taken Joshua in when he'd declined the hospitality of those who loved him, but who might no longer truly know him.

CHAPTER SEVEN

Hope could not think of Joshua Penrose as a lodger, no matter how hard she tried. He'd spent most of an afternoon hanging paper stars in the conservatory with Holly, while Hope had made a fine, uninterrupted start on Mrs. Colchester's second sampler. Joshua left a nightly bed of coals glowing in the conservatory hearth for the boys, and last night, Hope had heard muted laughter floating down the chimney.

At Joshua's suggestion, Hope had gone through Edwin's remaining wardrobe and left a selection of stockings, shoes, caps, and mufflers for the boys. Every item had been gone the next morning, and *Thak yu* had been lettered in the ash on the hearthstones. Hope hadn't been able to bring herself to pawn Edwin's wardrobe for pennies, but knowing his effects were put to use by children who truly needed them was wonderful.

When Mrs. Colchester's sampler was done, Hope's next sewing project would be taking in Edwin's shirts and waistcoats for boyish figures.

"I'm selling the seascapes," Joshua said one morning shortly before Christmas. "You will not tattle to Mr. Peters, because either you own these paintings or I do, and we both agree they should be sold."

He'd waited to raise this topic until Holly had gone out to the garden to make snow angels with Heifer. A mama appreciated that sort of discretion.

"I've never particularly liked them," Hope said, rather than argue with sound logic. "They are cold and vaguely threatening. Even the bright sunlight is harsh somehow. Let's wrap them up if you intend to haul them halfway across Town."

She led the way from the kitchen into the foyer, which was chilly, but no longer quite arctic.

Joshua took down the first painting, a scene of billowing waves, billowing clouds, and brilliant sunshine striking high, chalky cliffs.

"I wanted images of something other than some enormous ancestral pile set amid groomed acreage on a perfect English summer day. When I arrived in New York, it wasn't the English seacoast I missed, but rather, the thought of that verdant countryside."

"I miss my brother," Hope said, collecting the second painting—more rocks and waves and clouds. "We used to squabble like old hens, but now..."

"You miss him, and the ache is there, and you can't make it go away." Joshua took the painting from her and set it against the wall. "But you don't know if he's missing you or cursing your memory. Have you written to him recently?"

"Mr. Peters has tried. If the letter was addressed in my hand, it might be tossed directly into the fire. No luck."

"Try again. In your hand. If there's one source of correspondence I do not open with glee, it's the lot that comes from the lawyers. They might think he's dunning them to help with Edwin's debts."

"Edwin did not die in debt, thank heavens—other than the mortgage. You're sure you want to sell all three?"

Joshua had lined the paintings up next to one another at the base of the wall. They made a striking triptych, full of motion, sophisticated brushwork, and exquisite contrasts, but the images were lacking in warmth.

"Are *you* sure *you* want to sell all three?" Joshua asked, half hugging Hope with an arm around her shoulders." His tone was gently teasing, but his affectionate little squeeze suggested he knew how hard parting with any memento of happier times might be.

Even mementos Hope hadn't chosen and didn't particularly like. "Be off with you, and mind your footing. Where will you take them?"

"Knightsbridge," Joshua said, "is full of bachelors trying to make their rooms look civilized, unless much has changed in the past few years. The neighborhood is close enough to Mayfair that the goods on offer will be superior quality and far enough from Bond Street that one can browse in relative anonymity. If the gallery I bought them from is still in business, I'll give them first crack."

Hope slipped from his side rather than turn a half hug into the genuine article. She would never have known where to sell the paintings, nor have had the strength to carry all three any distance, or the means to hire a porter for the job.

Thus did poverty beget poverty, a reality Mr. Peters apparently had yet to grasp.

"I'll get an old sheet to wrap them in," Hope said, starting up the stairs. "They deserve at least that much protection from the elements."

When Joshua left with his seascapes, she went back to work on Mrs. Colchester's *Let There Be Light* sampler. The front parlor was actually warm, not merely bearable, and the curtains were drawn back rather than kept closed to hoard the heat.

"Warmth and light, the two greatest treasures at this time of year." Sustenance was to be valued as well, of course. Peace and quiet were near the top of the list too.

And all those affectionate little gestures—the hugs and squeezes of the hand or pats to the shoulder. Those were irresistibly sweet.

"Where's Joshua?" Holly bellowed her question from the parlor door. The cat hopped ahead of her and perched on the arm of the wing chair, looking about the room as if to pose the same query.

"Joshua has taken the seascapes from the front hallway to be sold."

Holly bounced into the wing chair. "Will Mr. Peters be mad? He was mad when you told him you'd sold the yellow palace picture."

Odd, that Holly's thoughts should go immediately to the solicitor's disapproval. "Mr. Peters's opinion on the matter doesn't signify. This house is full of art. A few pictures one way or another won't make that much of a difference."

Which is what Hope should have said to Mr. Peters when he'd grumbled about the house-scape being sold.

"When is Joshua coming back, Mama?"

"Before supper." Though a small, timid voice in Hope's head suggested his return was not a certainty. "I have an idea, Hollister Ann."

Heifer abandoned the arm of the chair and appropriated Holly's lap. "Are you zasperated with me?"

"I am not at all exasperated with you. Joshua agrees with me that you are a remarkably well-mannered child. I thought we might brighten up this room with a few camellias in a holiday bouquet."

"We could add some of the holly that Mrs. Winfield brought. I still have some red ribbon from the candles."

"Then let's be about it. We might also make a bouquet for the kitchen."

The suggested activity had the desired effect of distracting Holly from Joshua's absence, but not so for Hope.

He was nothing like a lodger. Lodgers were notorious for tracking mud onto the carpets, appearing tipsy at the front door late at night, and singing to attract the notice of every disapproving neighbor. Lodgers were late with their rent and unappreciative of their quarters or the lady whose hard work kept those quarters presentable.

Joshua was no sort of lodger.

"How many?" Holly asked as they surveyed a half-dozen bushes heavy with pink blooms. The hues ranged from nearly white to nearly scarlet, with every shade in between.

"Let's start with three blooms each," Hope said. "Just enough to be a treat for the eye and nose."

"We need a vase." Holly skipped over to the counter built along one wall. "We have lots of vases. Lots and lots. We also have lots of mouse poop. Is mouse poop good for anything?"

Children are so observant. "Mouse droppings are an excellent means of putting any self-respecting housekeeper in a temper. What have you there?"

Holly brought over two matching glass bud vases. Very simple, a bit dusty.

"We have lots of these in the cupboard. They need a good wash."

"That, they do..." Hope looked at the vases, at the bushes heavy with blooms, and at the cupboard Holly had left half open. "I have another idea, Hollister Ann, and we will need some clever boys to help us see this idea through."

"I only know our boys. I don't know any clever boys. Joshua is clever."

Joshua was clever, determined, patient with children, and kind... He was dear, entirely too huggable, and had an understated sense of humor.

"Our boys are very clever. Bundle up and fetch Gabriel, Slivers, or Buns for me, would you?"

"Buns is always outside the bakery looking skinny and cold. I'll fetch him."

While Hope waited for Joshua to return, she kept busy making little bouquets and sending the boys forth to sell them to holiday shoppers. When the vases ran out, Hope started on all the mismatched cups and mugs in the servants' pantry, and when the red ribbon ran out, strips of burlap tied in jaunty bows looked almost as festive.

Luncheon had come and gone, and the bushes were considerably less burdened with blossoms before Hope heard the front door open.

"That's Joshua!" Holly yelled, scampering from the conservatory. "I'll tell him we sold the flowers and made tons of money!"

A lady would not be caught dead celebrating such an accomplishment, but Hope's mood was nearly festive—also relieved.

"Perhaps I'm no lady," she murmured, taking the last of the bouquets with her. The blooms were reddish and white and a bit droopy, as camellias tended to be, but they were fresh flowers in December, and the light floral scent was gorgeous.

The feeling of having seen an opportunity and turning that opportunity into lucrative action was gorgeous as well. She'd followed Joshua's example rather than fretting over what Mr. Peters would think of handing over a lot of old dusty vases in exchange for coin.

"Mama, I told him!" Hope caroled. "I told Joshua we sold the flowers, and the boys helped, and now we have money."

Joshua, his cheeks ruddy, the toes of his boots damp, smiled down at Holly. "You also notified the neighbors for three houses in either direction of your brilliant industry. Might we spare my ears by lowering our voices a bit?"

"Yes," Holly said, spinning around. "I am happy. We sent a bouquet to Mrs. Colchester and the Colquitts for free. 'Holiday greetings, from Mrs. Burdette and Miss Burdette.'" Holly curtseyed extravagantly. "Buns said he will change his name to Loaves, because now he can buy a loaf of day-old bread instead of a day-old bun. Slivers said his name should be Loafs because he never does anything useful. They smacked each other, and Gabriel yelled at them."

"Thank you for the report," Joshua said, unbuttoning his greatcoat. "One does want to remain informed. Perhaps you could find a place in the kitchen for that lovely bouquet your mother is holding?"

"On the mantel, where Heifer can't knock it over!" Holly had abandoned any attempt to moderate her volume.

"Here you go," Hope said, passing over the vase. "Mind you don't let Heifer trip you on the steps."

Holly swiped the vase from her mother's hand. "Heifer never trips me. He only trips people he doesn't like. C'mon, Heffy-poo."

Girl and cat whisked off down the corridor, leaving a blessed, sweet quiet in their wake.

Joshua stepped closer at the same time Hope moved toward him. The hug was natural, spontaneous, and as precious as all the previous hugs Hope had shared with Joshua.

This time, she let the embrace shift from a hug to a mutual holding. "You were gone for some time."

"Went chasing after my trunks, which apparently reside in some dockside warehouse, awaiting the dray I'm to send to fetch them at my own expense."

"At least somebody knows where they are. We did make some money today."

Joshua peered down at her. "Enterprising of you. Will you be insulted if I say I'm proud of you? The bouquet was quite pretty, and fresh flowers are an unexpected treat this time of year."

He was *proud of her*. How long had it been since Hope had been proud of herself? She leaned against him, absorbing both the compliment and the balm to her soul.

"I missed you." Where those words had come from, Hope did not know. "Fretted that you would not come back." Just as Holly had.

"That I'd steal the paintings and disappear? If I disappear, Hope Burdette, I will first pay what I owe you."

He stepped back and withdrew a pouch of coins from the pocket of his greatcoat. "Seascapes are apparently all the rage, and an artist whose work I happened to like years ago has rocketed to fashionable popularity." He put the whole sack in Hope's hand and whispered a number into her ear. "That's your half. Have a look."

Hope opened the sack and beheld a small hoard of sovereigns. Not small change, not small anythings. Beautiful, bright golden sovereigns.

"This cannot be right."

"What isn't right is for you and Holly to shiver and fret your way through the holidays. That is the amount you are owed for those paintings, and I kept the same for myself."

Sovereigns. "To think, all this time, I've been late on my mortgage payments, scrimping, and scrounging, counting lumps of sugar..." Relief washed through Hope, leaving her blinking and unaccountably weak-kneed. "We can have plum pudding."

She could also afford coach fare home to her family, if worse came to worst. A weight of fear and anxiety slid away, and breathing came more easily.

Sovereigns.

Joshua hugged her again, gently resting his chin on her crown. "We can have plum pudding and play snapdragon and exchange tokens. We might even, if we're feeling particularly jolly, sing a few carols or hang some mistletoe here and there."

Mistletoe, as in merriment and celebration and...

Hope kissed him on the mouth. "We might. We might at that." She'd intended the kiss as another gesture of affection and joy, not an overture to seduction, but intentions had a way of lurking at the edges of the heart, and when Joshua brushed his lips over hers, romance certainly joined the affray.

He knew how to kiss, did Joshua Penrose. How to kiss and flirt and tempt. Hope hadn't had any use for the same skills in quite some time, but moment by joyous moment, they were coming back to her, and soon, she was giving as good as she got.

And then some.

~

What are you doing? What in the name of Gaspar, Melchior, and Balthasar are you doing?

This time, the exasperated voice in Joshua's head belonged to Joshua's grandpapa, who'd been a jolly soul, but not blessed with abundant patience where wayward boys were concerned.

And the answer was simple: *I am kissing a woman whom I esteem and desire, and she is kissing me back.*

The result of that activity was glorious. Joshua had forgotten the sheer joy of an exuberant kiss, the leaping of the blood, the quickening of the heart. The wonderful knowledge that desire had not abandoned him for all time, that an estimable woman found him attractive.

Hope eased her mouth away and rested her forehead on Joshua's chest. "Who needs mistletoe?"

We do. Badly. "A curious tradition. Perhaps the idea with mistletoe is to prevent indiscriminate kissing in myriad locations and limit the enthusiasms to doorways and foyers?"

She peeked up at him. "I fear that's not quite how it works. Having kissed you once, properly, or improperly, the mistletoe will adorn my thoughts even if it's not in evidence in the house."

"And yet," Joshua said, "you might have to turn me out onto the street come the New Year. This is getting a bit complicated, isn't it?"

Hope moved away enough to finish unbuttoning his greatcoat. "Will you turn me out if Edwin's purchase of the home can somehow be invalidated?"

The house was Joshua's. His sole legacy from Grandpapa, the refuge he'd crossed an ocean for. Hope was... not Joshua's. As if some angel had whacked him on the shoulder with a copper soup ladle, his well-kissed imagination presented the possibility that he could have both—Hope and the house, Holly and Heifer, happily—for the most part—ever after.

Joshua wasn't as keen on having a conservatory full of pickpockets, but enterprising young fellows could change careers from time to time.

"You are having to think about this," Hope said, hanging his coat on a hook. "You were supposed to say, 'I could never take the roof over your head, much less over Holly's.' But you didn't say that.'"

She sounded more disappointed than offended.

"And you did not say to me, 'Joshua, you will always have a place in my household,' because we agreed to a truce only, not an eternal alliance. Do you regret kissing me?"

Her gaze went to the portrait of jolly old Grandpapa. "I should. I most assuredly do not. The situation is confusing."

"For both of us. I do not regret kissing you, but there's something you should know."

She twisted the lock on the front door and made a *say on* gesture with her hand.

"I went to see my solicitor as I was rambling about Town. His offices were on my route to the docks, and he was alerted to the possibility of my return. I expected him to open the house for me and wanted to know what had become of my instructions."

"This is Mr. Chumley?"

"The very one. He clerked for Grandpapa, and now Chumley is a senior partner in a solicitor's practice. I trust him implicitly, but he's apparently off to the shires to dandle grandchildren and neglect his correspondence. The senior clerk explained that my letter was personal, so nobody opened it."

Hope ran a finger along the sideboard and examined the tip. Burning coal steadily in only two hearths could make for a constant need to dust.

"Go on."

"That's the whole tale. I sought out my solicitor, and he's out of the office until the New Year." Well, no, it wasn't quite the whole tale. "The next time I speak with Chumley, I'd like you to be with me."

"Why?"

"Because..." Joshua took Hope's hand. "I want you to hear the same evidence I do. I want you to have the opportunity to interrogate old Chumley as thoroughly as I will. I could never leave you and Holly homeless. I promise you that. My cash reserves at this point amount to less than one hundred and fifty pounds, assuming I can pawn what's in my trunks, but I have some means, Hope, and I do not abandon my friends."

Holly might point out that he'd abandoned friends to travel to New York, and she'd be... somewhat right.

"You have means," Hope said, worrying a nail. "I have a mortgage. Only owners have mortgages, Joshua."

"True in the usual case." Which this might not be. Joshua considered dropping to one knee and requesting permission to embark on a courtship. Hope would think he'd lost his wits, and she might be somewhat right there too.

"Are you concerned that I might leave you homeless?" Hope asked, easing her hand from his.

"I have friends in London who will offer me hospitality if need be, though I would rather not impose on them. You must not worry about my physical safety." And having called at the solicitor's office, albeit Joshua's personal solicitor, word of Joshua's return might soon reach those friends.

"I wouldn't turn you out," Hope said. "Holly and Heifer would never speak to me again, and I would be hard put to speak to myself."

"Our truce holds?" Even as Joshua asked the question, he knew they already had more than a truce. Walking back across the City, he had noticed his mind had run along the lines of *wonder what's for supper* and *which story will Holly want tonight*.

He'd not been returning to his house, he'd been returning to his *home*, and the difference lay in the woman who'd tried to evict him a few short days ago.

"Our truce holds," Hope said, "though our situation grows more complicated, and if you would not mind, I'd like you present when I talk to Mr. Peters too."

Did she but know it, Hope had just taken a step beyond truce and toward that alliance Joshua had mentioned.

"I would be honored," Joshua said, "to escort you on any calls, business or personal."

"What of the kissing?" Hope asked, glancing up at a crossbeam perfectly positioned to hold a sprig of mistletoe. "Was that an error in judgment?"

"I was honored by the kissing too," Joshua said. "And I do not now, nor will I ever, regard kissing you as a misstep of any kind. I wasn't sure I would ever..."

Hope nodded. "I wasn't either. Wasn't sure it mattered. Do you know something else?"

Please say you'd like to kiss me again. "What else?"

"I am relieved that your solicitor wasn't in. I want this Yuletide calm, Joshua Penrose. I want a few days of peace and plenty, of merriment and rejoicing. I intend to have them."

Will you have me? Rather than ask that question, Joshua wrestled with the notion that he was to become Hope's first venture in the direction of merry widowhood. She was attracted to him, he was convenient, and he was apparently willing, except...

No, he was not capable of dalliance. Not yet, maybe never again.

"We have our truce, then," Joshua said. "Peace and plenty, and no thought for what the New Year might bring, unless it's a happy thought."

"And a few sprigs of mistletoe might liven up the old place considerably. I'd better start supper." Hope swished off down the corridor, leaving a ringing silence in her wake.

Joshua wasn't sure what exactly had shifted between him and Hope, though he was fairly certain the shift had been in a positive direction. He was equally certain that *the old place* would indeed benefit from a few dozen tastefully displayed sprigs of mistletoe.

CHAPTER EIGHT

"It's Christmas Eve," Holly said, "and they have been good boys. We should leave them tokens for tomorrow."

Hope put the last of her pear tart on Holly's plate. "Had this generous impulse come sooner, we might have acted on it more easily."

Hope had awakened that morning to find that the boys had tidied the conservatory from corner to corner and floor to ceiling. The makeshift hen pen had been raked within an inch of its birdie life, and burlap sacks had been folded under fresh straw in the nesting boxes.

The biddies had never looked more content, and they'd gifted the household with four eggs since their quarters had been refurbished by the elves.

"The hens have been good too," Joshua said, pushing his empty plate aside. "What does a hen consider an appropriate gesture of appreciation?"

He had the knack of engaging Holly's imagination, a challenge Hope had lost track of somewhere between stitching samplers, fretting over coal, and remitting sums to Mr. Peters.

"They love apple cores," Holly said, disappearing the pear tart. "Mama, can we feed the girls some apples?"

Hope pretended to consider the matter, though a week ago, the answer would have been a firm, grim, no.

"One," she said, "and we will cut it up in tiny pieces so even Helga will get a few nibbles." Helga wasn't picked on so much as she was shy. Holly had given her a battle maiden's name in hopes of inspiring the hen's self-confidence.

"They will be so happy! I'm going to write a poem about Christmas chickens." Holly had half scrambled off the bench before she came about, sat squarely, and looked Hope in the eye. "Mama, the meal was delicious. May I please be excused to write some poetry?"

"You may be excused. Why don't you take a stab at sonnet form?"

Holly looked between the adults in puzzlement. "Sonnet form?"

"Make it rhyme," Joshua said. "We'll explain meter and other subtleties later. First, make it rhyme, and I know of not one word that rhymes with Helga."

Holly was up the stairs like a Congreve rocket. "Elga, belga, celga, delga. Delta almost rhymes. Elga, felga, gelga..." She closed the door at the top of the steps decisively, leaving the kitchen in blessed quiet.

"I had not realized," Hope said, "how subdued Holly had been growing. She has her father's exuberant nature, but she was losing it. She will work at her poem until she falls asleep." By the nice, cozy fire in the parlor.

What a difference a few days in the right company could make. What a difference selling a few paintings...

"Have another pear tart," Joshua said. "I'll do the dishes. I thought we might leave the boys some cider and shortbread, if nothing else. I bought cinnamon shortbread on my way back from the posting inn."

"I saw that. You will note that I did not snitch a single bite." The scent of fresh, buttery shortbread had been tempting, though.

Joshua rose from the bench, swung the kettle over the coals, and began clearing the table. His tasks were mundane, but that Hope allowed him to simply get on with the job while she sat and nibbled a second half of a tart...

His image grew watery.

"Hope Burdette, are you crying?" He was immediately straddling the bench beside her. "Why on earth would you be lachrymose when we are in anticipation of the first sonnet in the history of English literature on the topic of holiday hens?"

"I am trying not to cry, precisely because that happy honor awaits us. She hasn't written a poem for months, Joshua. I have had more gingerbread in the past three days than in the entire previous holiday season. You shoveled the walks, you tend to the mail, you look after Holly and the boys. You do d-dishes."

He hugged Hope and passed over his handkerchief—clean, probably from the one smallish trunk that had arrived the previous day—then rose and swung the kettle off the fire before it began whistling. Next, he took peppermint sachets out of the tea drawer that was full for the first time in months and put together a tray.

"You darn my socks," he said. "You make lentil soup that isn't too salty, a feat even the great Carême could not emulate. You saw half a dozen boys properly wrapped up against the elements, probably for the first time in their little misspent lives. You feed me when I'd pretty much forgotten why I'm supposed to eat. Shall we join Holly in the parlor?"

"We shall not. Set the dishes to soak, and I'll pour out."

The weepy moment had passed, but the feelings had not. Gratitude, of course, because Hope's holidays were turning out much warmer and sweeter than she'd anticipated, but also bewilderment—and more than a little resentment.

"You sold three paintings, Joshua, and my whole outlook has shifted. Why didn't I sell every sketch and landscape in the place?"

"Mr. Peters advised against it." Joshua brought the tray to the table. "You were grateful for his advice. Now you suspect him of incompetence?"

"Blindness, perhaps. He sees the pitiful state of my finances, sees how I struggle to pay the mortgage. The most frequent advice J. Bartholomew Peters has dispensed is that I am to be patient. It's impossible to be patient when the hens aren't laying, and your child is hungry."

Joshua fixed her tea with a dash of honey, another little luxury, and he'd used just the right amount.

"You did not tell me your brother dwells in Weybridge, Hope. I could walk that distance in less than a day if the roads were fair."

Twenty miles or so and half a world away. "Orson might have moved. I have no way of knowing." He probably had more children. He and Alma had both wanted a large family. "If he doesn't reply, I will try writing to his wife. Alma has the biggest heart. She'd toss Gabriel and his minions into the nearest laundry tub, scrub them silly, and turn them into proper schoolboys, all the while stuffing them with good cooking and dressing them in sturdy clothes."

"They would not thank her for that trip through the suds. I prefer the incremental-bribery approach when negotiating with barbarians." Joshua sipped his tea as if seriously considering how to civilize half a dozen junior criminals. "Very little a boy won't do for sweets or stories. I bought them a volume of Aesop."

"That was the parcel in the pantry with the shortbread?"

"It was. Gabriel is literate. He can read to his friends. Why haven't you written to Alma previously?"

Hope held her mug in her hands, relishing the warmth. "Fear, I suppose. I have become such a fearful creature—afraid of losing my house, of losing Holly, of losing my wits and my dignity... And the more fearful one is, the less one can see the solutions at hand—sell the paintings, look high and low for a fresh stash of coal, ask for a bit in advance for the next sampler, trade the boys stockings for some chores. I was not helpless, but I felt..."

"Overwhelmed and alone," Joshua said, stroking his fingers over

Hope's wrist. "Too aware that any action can end up being a mistake."

"A disaster."

The pause in the discussion was reflective and peaceful. Hope waited to speak again because she suspected Joshua was also ruminating about choices.

"I sent a note today to my friends, Hope. If you have the fortitude to contact your brother directly, after all his silence and indifference, I can at least let old friends know of my safe arrival."

"Was that hard?"

He nodded. "Shouldn't have been, but these are people who never knew Maureen, who knew me for years before I even made her acquaintance. They know the version of me that was never married."

"Happily married people," Hope muttered, infusing a little ire into her tone. "Of all the nerve."

Joshua smiled, a sweet, genuine, conspiratorial smile that yet held a bit of rue. "You have restored my courage, Hope Burdette. Courage has been your Christmas gift to me, and I have never had any finer holiday present."

She caught his fingers in her own. "Likewise, Joshua Penrose. I am braver for having made your acquaintance." Also happier, warmer, and better fed. She would be sad to part from him at the New Year, if part she must, but stronger for having shared the holidays with him. "Why did we never get around to hanging any mistletoe?"

Joshua's smile transformed into an expression a bit more mischievous. "For my part, I did not dare."

Hope considered that smile and considered their joined hands and considered… what she wanted for Christmas.

More warmth, more joy, *more Joshua*, while she still had his company. Widows, provided they were discreet, were *allowed*. All of society agreed on that much.

"We don't need the mistletoe," Hope said, rising. "Holly will be absorbed with her poem until Twelfth Night. We have both been very good for a very long time. Let's be brave, shall we?"

He got to his feet. "We ought to discuss the metes and bounds of this bravery, Hope. I am not one to undertake intimacies lightly."

Hope came around the table and wrapped him in a hug. "Neither am I."

She could feel him considering, weighing, pondering, even as he rubbed her back in a languorous rhythm that made her bones and her heart melt.

"You're sure?" he asked, hands going still. "You aren't in the grip of an overabundance of gingerbread or toddies?"

They were saving the toddy makings for tomorrow. "I am of age, so are you, and my mind is made up."

"And full of mistletoe." He kissed her nose. "Very well, but we will talk of next steps and expectations when the moment is right."

Hope kissed him back—on the mouth. She did not much care what cautions or reminders he wanted to reiterate regarding the house. They would not turn each other out, and beyond that, Hope was more interested in seizing the day *and the man* than investigating the legalities.

The house was hers. She knew that. She wished the man was hers as well, but she would settle for having him all to herself for the next hour.

She'd try to settle for that much, anyway.

~

A request to embark on a courtship should stand alone, untethered from holidays, family occasions, and other distractions. As Joshua ran the warmer over the sheets of Hope's bed, he realized that he also wanted this courtship to commence free of the grief that Maureen's and Eric's deaths had cast over Yuletide in the past.

The New Year was soon enough for stirring declarations and rehearsed speeches, assuming Hope would like to hear them.

As certain as Joshua was that he wanted a future with her, he was not certain of *her*. A similar, nigh instant conviction had befallen him with Maureen, but she'd leapt to let him know his sentiments were reciprocated.

"You're sure?" Hope asked, sitting at the rickety vanity. "I don't want to impose."

"Impose." Joshua nearly burst out laughing. "Madam, you may impose upon me as often and passionately as ever you wish. You have imposed laughter, affection, trust, physical safety from the elements, kindness, a few tart lectures, and some delicious cooking on me. The mind boggles and the heart reels to consider what manner of imposition you might contemplate in this bed."

"You mean that." She began removing pins from her hair. "I do believe you mean that."

The pins went into a small tin that had probably held soap or tea.

Joshua watched the little ritual Edwin Burdette would never see again. He hoped the brilliant inventor had appreciated the sheer domestic loveliness of a woman taking down her hair before bed. Joshua had, for a time, then Maureen's nightly routine had become merely that, as his quotidian going-to bed sequence had for her.

He put his hands on Hope's shoulders. "Allow me, please."

She nodded, and Joshua searched out the last of the pins, undid her braid, and brushed her hair into a shiny auburn cascade down her back.

What ensued after he'd refashioned her braid was not a jolly romp, and neither was it the height of amatory virtuosity on anybody's part. Hope was ticklish, Joshua sneezed at a particularly inopportune moment, and laughter limned desire with a tenderness neither party had expected.

Or perhaps they had foreseen the dangerous advent of that tenderness and had known enough to be cautious as a result.

That Christmas Eve, there might not have been peace on earth, but in Hope's bed, there was joy and pleasure. Joshua allowed himself to believe there might also have been love, for the love was certainly present in his heart.

Christmas had been a gray, bitterly cold day that had thrown into greater relief the indulgence of toddies, a memorable dinner of roast goose courtesy of the chop shop, and a sizable serving of plum pudding. Christmas night was concluding in the kitchen, with Joshua, Hope, and Holly gathered around a deck of cards at the worktable.

For Hope, taking Joshua to bed had changed much... and little. He was still the dear, patient man who'd left the largest plums for Holly to pluck in her first game of snapdragon, plums he'd just happened to place at the very edge of the shallow bowl of flaming brandy. He still had a fine baritone singing voice and a faulty memory for the proper lyrics of the Christmas carols.

While shepherds washed their socks by night...

Joshua was also Hope's lover. He sent her brooding looks and naughty smiles at odd moments and inspired her to stare at nothing while fending off memories of laughter, pleasure, and an aching sense of homecoming.

"Mama is thinking again," Holly said, picking up a card. "She thinks she ought to be working on Mrs. Colchester's sampler."

"That project is nearly finished," Hope replied as Holly turned over a seven and a nine, then placed them facedown again. "Amazing how much can be accomplished while you and Joshua practiced pitching snowballs at the garden wall."

"Holly has good aim." Joshua studied the cards covering the kitchen table. "The next step will be hitting a nonstationary object." He turned over two sevens. "Lucky, lucky me."

Said in all innocence, with a lowering of his lashes that held a stocking-full of innuendo.

"I vote you serve as Holly's first moving target. You are very fit and have excellent stamina." Amazing stamina.

"Quite a compliment, coming from one who boasts plenty of the same gift."

"Mama, choose your cards."

Hope turned over the nine and three.

"My turn!" Holly crowed.

And thus Christmas night proceeded, until several eternities later, bedtime for Holly arrived. When Hope had duly tucked her daughter in, the child demanded a story from Joshua, who claimed he was too tired to read, leaving Hope to do the voices for Androcles and the Lion.

"Next Christmas, I want a lion," Holly murmured, eyes closing. "And a unicorn, because the unicorn is the only creature in the whole forest who can tame the lion." She yawned contentedly, turned on her side, and promptly dropped off to sleep.

Joshua remained in the rocking chair, and Hope sat on the corner of the bed.

"How is it," she said, "that I have barely stirred from this house all day, and I am nearly too tired to rise?"

Joshua stood and offered his hand. "The holidays are wearying, but we've made it through Christmas Day. The carols have been sung, the feast consumed, and the tokens exchanged. The rest isn't as difficult."

He slipped an arm around Hope's shoulders, and they returned to the kitchen in a companionable accord that nonetheless held a thread of awareness.

"Holly loves her sketchbook." Hope loved that Joshua had chosen the gift so thoughtfully. He'd even included colored pencils and erasers and a few sticks of charcoal.

"Holly loves easily and often. I love my stockings."

Stockings were a quick and simple knitting project, and Hope had sworn Holly to secrecy about them. Hope had embellished

Joshua's holiday gift with stitched mistletoe and made him try them on for Holly to admire.

Pure silliness. The best gift of the day, besides warmth, a full belly, and companionship, had been the laughter.

Though the flirtation had been lovely too.

"I don't believe you are pondering another round of cards, Mrs. Burdette." Joshua shifted so his arms were draped over her shoulders. "Do you like your gloves?"

A pair for out of doors, exquisitely stitched, fur-lined, a perfect fit. "Love them. I want to wear them in the house."

"They are not enough," Joshua said, drawing her against his chest. "I expected to endure the holidays, Hope, but with you, I have found celebration, and I was long overdue for celebration."

Hope heard those words as the gift they were meant to be, but also as a prelude to parting. She was unready and unwilling to allow that parting to begin so soon.

"If you can manage to remain awake a bit longer, I thought I'd join you in the parlor before turning in."

His embrace subtly shifted, becoming more relaxed and intimate. "Please do join me, for as long as you can."

The whole business took some ingenuity and a bit of maneuvering of furniture, but the joy and the pleasure were worth it. Hope fell asleep snuggled up to Joshua's chest, with visions dancing in her head of him wearing nothing but a pair of socks.

She woke in her own bed to a brilliant sunny morning, the eaves dripping with sparkling icicles. Joshua's voice came from the laundry, Holly's dubious soprano joining him in a verse of "Adeste Free Daylilies."

As Hope dressed for the day, it occurred to her that the loving had been sweet and languid, and in that, too, she had felt a sense of impending goodbye.

"Behold, I am shorn of my whiskers," Joshua said, coming into the kitchen, Holly capering at his right, Heifer strutting to his left. "Mademoiselle Holly has declared me presentable for one more day.

Happy Boxing Day." He kissed Hope on the cheek, bringing with him a whiff of his cedar shaving soap. "Do you ladies have plans for this morning?"

"Mama, do we have plans?" Holly grabbed Joshua's hand. "Will we go calling?"

"I hadn't really thought..." Hope *had* thought. She'd thought and wished and even daydreamed about Joshua making Boxing Day calls with her and Holly, a little makeshift family observing a tradition that had been neglected in recent years.

"Take some camellias," Joshua said, swinging the kettle over the coals. "They refuse to stop blooming. In fact, I might collect a few before I go out myself."

Holly dropped his hand. "Where are you going?"

Oh, exactly. Where was he going, and why must he go there without them? Unfair questions. A holiday truce was not an oath of allegiance.

"Holly, we are not to pry. Perhaps you could choose some fresh flowers for us to take to Mrs. Colchester?"

"If we must call on Mrs. Colchester," Holly retorted, "I want Joshua to come with us. He is our *lodger*." In Holly's lexicon, that apparently elevated him to the status of permanent family fixture.

"If you can wait until later in the day," Joshua said, "I will be happy to accompany you. The truth is, I have an apology to make to some friends who have probably worried about me. I want to have a Christmas token or two in hand when I make that call, and I have not yet found anything appropriate. I thought I'd nose through the shops on my way to Mayfair."

Mayfair? The most exclusive neighborhood in London?

Holly glowered up at him. "If they are your friends, you say sorry and don't make them worry about you again."

Joshua knelt down. "I have not seen them for years, Hollister Ann. They missed me, and after a time, I barely wrote to them. A simple 'sorry' won't do."

She wrinkled her nose. "Are they mad at you?"

Joshua rose. "Likely, they are, but they are too kind to show it. I have behaved badly."

"Will they act all zasperated and call you Joshua Ann when you try to apologize?"

"Something along those lines. Might you wait for me to join you on some afternoon calls?"

"Mama, can we wait?"

"We can wait, and make bouquets, and maybe draw some flower sketches to give to our neighbors."

"Ohhhh, sketches!" Holly pelted up the steps. Stopped halfway along the staircase and turned. "Don't forget to say sorry. You have to *say* it."

"And never disappear on them again," Joshua murmured, half smiling. "You are raising a formidable female there, Mrs. Burdette."

Holly closed the door at the top of the steps with a decisive bang. Heifer took up his post on the warm hearth.

"I'd go with you if you asked me to," Hope said. "Mrs. Belchamp wouldn't mind watching Holly for a couple hours." She would not mind much.

Joshua took the kettle off the fire. "If you came along, Jane would make a lovely fuss over you—as well she should—and recruit you onto one of her charitable committees, have your whole life history in a quarter hour, and send you home with a basket of treats sufficient to spoil every meal until Lady Day. The rest of the conversation would be about the weather on my crossing, the weather today, and the hope for an early spring."

"You know them well."

"They know me well, which was part of the problem. I will lose my nerve if you come with me, and then I will eat too many anise biscuits just to keep my mouth occupied."

"Easy to do." *My love goes with you.* Hope didn't say that, though it was true. "Grief can derange us in little ways. The little ways all add up and befuddle even those who love us. I expect your friends know this."

"*You* know it. That has mattered to me a great deal, Hope Ann."

She busied herself at the window box. The last time he'd called her Hope Ann, she'd been flat on her back, smiling dazedly into the darkness.

"You need not make this pilgrimage on an empty stomach." She extracted cheese, eggs, milk, and butter from the chilly depths of the window box. "The thrilling prospect of tea with Mrs. Colchester means you won't tarry among your friends."

"The thrilling prospect of escorting you and Holly about the neighborhood means I will certainly hurry home." Joshua set about slicing bread for toast, which he did particularly well.

Breakfast was on the table shortly thereafter, a coordinated task that resulted in fluffy omelets, golden toast, hot tea, and sliced oranges.

What a difference a bit of coin had made.

What a difference Joshua's company made.

"Let's leave the artist undisturbed for a few more moments," Joshua said, settling on the bench. "For what we are about to receive and for the peace and quiet with which we receive it, we are pathetically grateful."

Hope took the opposite bench with a murmured amen and tucked into her meal.

"Excellent omelet," Joshua said between bites.

"Perfect toast." And thus it went, but between *might I have the salt* and *would you like more jam*, Hope came to a realization.

If she had to choose between the house or a future with Joshua Penrose, the house, which she'd scrimped and fretted and lost months of sleep trying to preserve, would not be her first pick.

The house was a dwelling, shelter from the elements and a fixed abode. Certainly important in anybody's life.

But if she lived in the finest palace on earth without Joshua, Hope would miss him more than any fancy art, elegant molding, or imported wallpaper.

Much more.

CHAPTER NINE

The sensation came again, stronger than Joshua had felt it before. He was being followed, and the follower did not care if his presence was detected. Not a footpad, on this sparkling, bustling Boxing Day. Not a thief, but rather...

Ah. Of course. One who had the arcane skills of a street criminal, but no longer exercised them for nefarious ends.

Joshua strolled around a corner, ducked into the doorway of a chandler's shop, and waited. Half a minute later, a slim, dark-haired fellow teetering between youth and manhood sauntered around the corner as well. His appearance was nevertheless something of a shock.

"You've grown up, Neddy Wentworth." He'd grown civilized in addition to taller, more muscular, and exquisitely groomed. Ned of Newgate had become Ned of Bond Street, though a lurking wariness about the eyes betrayed a past the finest tailor could not disguise.

"You've come home, Joshua Penrose." Ned studied him with a seriousness the boy had lacked. "Or you've returned to England. Jane and Quinn are worried witless about you."

Foot traffic swirled around them, the chandler's shop bell tinkled in the sunny air, and an annoyance of boys was having a snowball fight over, between, and around the wheeled vehicles on the thoroughfare.

The conversation with Ned was utterly predictable—of course Quinn and Jane were worried, of course Ned would scold. Even as a boy in filthy, tattered attire, he'd been prodigiously talented as a conscience-at-large and not shy about exercising his office.

And yet, Joshua still felt a sense of unreality, as if he'd gone too many days without eating and had trouble distinguishing the products of his wandering wits from true earthly experiences.

"I am on my way to call on Their Graces," Joshua said as the bell went on tinkling and a stray snowball caused a coach horse to shy. "These are for Jane." He gestured with his bouquet of camellias that Holly had helped him arrange and Hope had discreetly rearranged.

Hope and Holly were real. Ned was... taking some getting used to.

"And here I thought those were for me. Come along, then, and you'd best have an explanation for why you waited until after Christmas to pay this call. The weather has been miserable, your absence has hung over the household like a foul miasma. I have been forced to consume so many anise biscuits to keep Cook's spirits up that I will swear off them for the next year."

"I told Quinn I would return by the New Year." A weak argument, at best.

"And in typical fashion, His Grace knew the instant your ship was spotted in the Pool. You do not send a note. You do not pop by after a good sleep and a wash. You can't be bothered to—"

"The holidays are a trying time for me, Ned." This discussion was trying as well. Ned the young man looked well on his way to a career as a solicitor or even a barrister, of all the ironies, and he'd be very good at cross-examination.

"The holidays are a trying time for many of us. Those of us shivering in church doorways, for example. A surfeit of London's relatively unfresh winter air does little for one's *joie de vivre*." His French accent was perfect.

He flipped a coin to a crossing sweeper, who tipped his cap and grinned.

"I take your point," Joshua said as the next section of street grew wider, the snowball fight fell behind, and the shops grew more elegant. "Now imagine that it's Christmas, the time of year when your worst, most unimaginable nightmare has been visited upon you. You are doing your best to put the past behind you, but your best is a feeble effort."

Ned, who usually had a comment ready for any occasion, remained silent.

"Then imagine," Joshua went on, "that you are invited to spend the holidays in close proximity to people who are happily sharing what had been your fondest dream. The dream you thought you had earned, but saw dashed to pieces in the cruelest possible way. They will try to understand the burden you carry, but they cannot."

"Quinn and Jane aren't as..."

"Yes?"

"Oblivious as they used to be. Not as heedless." Said with a certain stoic patience.

"I am not as heedless as I used to be either, and, Ned, I miss that ability to ignore what annoyed me or made me sad. I miss it a lot."

They turned another corner and beheld the snowy expanse of Hyde Park.

"No, you don't, Joshua Penrose. You don't miss that fellow who was in some ways a fool, for all he was a happy fool. Tell me about Mrs. Burdette."

Of course Ned would have done his homework, but at least he'd left off lecturing.

The bank relied on Ned's acumen in human affairs, and he had raised a natural intelligence-gathering instinct to a high art. Quinn's letters suggested he was very proud of Ned and more than a little worried for him.

"Hope Burdette is a widow who thinks her late husband bought the house where I am dwelling. I am nearly certain I did not sell it. We have agreed to settle our legal differences after the New Year."

"You've turned the front parlor into a bedroom, then?"

How could he...? Joshua took the length of four shops to puzzle it out. The chimneys. The kitchen and conservatory accounted for one plume of smoke, and the parlor was the second. No candles had been lit above the ground floor. Therefore...

"I have. We're conserving coal. I arrived in the middle of the latest storm, without English coin and without my trunks. Still don't have much blunt in hand."

Ned snorted. "If you were truly wealthy, you'd have none at all. You'd go through your whole week without sight of tuppence, and yet, somehow, you'd spend and get a fortune. It's magic."

The holidays were apparently a challenge for Ned as well. He tossed another coin to another crossing sweeper and got the same jaunty nod. How many crossing sweepers were dependent on Ned's casual charity?

"What about the girl?" Ned asked a bit too casually. "Holly."

"Hollister Ann is blessed with a devoted mother. She's very bright, somewhat forward, and needs more challenges." Also a pony, some siblings, tutors, frequent doses of country air, books, a patch of the garden to work as her own...

"You spent Christmas with strangers. Jane and Quinn won't understand that."

"I spent Christmas at home, Ned, and all I can do is apologize for not sending Jane and Quinn word of my return. I assume you told them where to find me?"

"You assume correctly, but every time the knocker sounds on the front door, Jane exchanges a hopeful look with His Grace. His Grace is set to pummel you if you don't show yourself soon."

"He still engages in fisticuffs?"

"Of course not. His Grace decimates with a lifted eyebrow, passes sentence with a silence, and condemns with polite commonplaces. All the lads at the bank practice imitating him. Jane has made quite the duke out of our Quinn, and he's good at it."

"Is he happy?"

Ned paused to allow a roaming dog of no particular pedigree to sniff his glove. The beast was thin, not starving. Not a stray, in other words.

"If Jane is happy, Quinn is happy, and conversely. I think Stephen moved out in part to be spared the daily sight of such bliss."

Stephen being Quinn's younger brother and the present ducal heir. Lord Stephen Wentworth, in point of fact. Two sisters rounded out the family portrait. Formidable women who suffered neither fools nor fortune hunters.

"Do you recall any mention of me selling my town house while I was a traveling, Ned?" Ned's formidable memory was rooted in years before he'd been taught to read. He could accurately sketch nearly anything he'd seen and repeat short conversations verbatim.

"None. I thought it ridiculous you didn't rent the place out and asked old Chumley about it once over a pint. A lovely house like that could bring in hundreds of pounds a year leased to the gentry on their annual rounds. Chum said that place is like your family seat, and you would no more rent it out than you would swear a vow of celibacy."

Odd comparison, given that Joshua had, until recently, been prepared for indefinite celibacy. "What do you know of a solicitor named J. Bartholomew Peters?"

The dog moved on, and Ned watched him trot through the holiday throng. "Bad actor, that one. A few years ago, there was some donnybrook over him watching the Society pages to see who had left for extended travel. He aimed for the families who shut up their London properties rather than rent them. Too high in the instep to be seen as a landlord, not high enough to keep the properties staffed during a long absence."

A sinking feeling joined the day's already-full complement of emotions. "Let me guess. He presents himself as the property agent and rents the houses out to the unsuspecting, collecting rent all the while and then canceling the lease when the owners are on the way home. Has anybody put notice of my return in the papers yet?"

"Neither Jane nor Quinn would allow that. It's for you to say when you've come home."

Quinn and Jane had doubtless wanted to see in what condition Joshua presented himself before announcing that he was once again biding in London. Prudent of them, and thoughtful.

"Well, keep mum, if you can. I suspect Mr. Peters is swindling Mrs. Burdette in very grand fashion. Her husband bought the house, if you can call it that, after he'd fallen ill, but Mrs. Burdette has been told there's also a mortgage on it."

"I can have a look around if you like. Mortgages require documents and loans and such like."

"Please have a thorough look around. If my suspicions are accurate, Mr. Peters is overdue for a very large lump of coal."

"He was caught before," Ned said as they crossed to Park Lane. "Best as I recall, it all blew over as a misunderstanding, meaning nobody wanted the scandal of legal repercussions. A pity, when here he is, preying on widows and all."

"You will not resort to the law of the knife, Ned."

"Mr. Penrose, surely you jest. Stephen is much better with knives than I could ever hope to be."

Every member of the Wentworth family was competent with knives. By now, even Jane might have picked up the skill.

The graceful façade of the Wentworth ducal abode came into view, tastefully bedecked with greenery and wreaths, a bright red bow adorning the knocker.

"Jane might cry," Ned said, the stoicism once again audible. "His Grace hates it when Jane cries." Ned apparently dreaded Jane's lachrymosity as well.

Joshua thought of Hope, weepy, fierce, and sweet. "His Grace will simply have to endure, because when I lay eyes on the pair of them, I might shed a few tears myself."

Ned looked over at him sharply, as if such an admission might be proof of inchoate witlessness, but as Joshua beheld the stately house, the cheery decorations, and the curious relief unweighting his heart, he knew that some tears were simply evidence of humanity in all its wonderful, messy glory.

"Lead on, Ned, and try not to hog all the biscuits."

"You are home," Jane said for the third time. "You are finally, finally home." She hugged Joshua to her with shameless desperation and reveled in his cedary scent. Had he been her own brother, she could not have been more pleased and relieved to see him.

Though he was too skinny, and his embrace was more careful than it should have been. Didn't those wretched Americans know how to look after a grieving widower?

"Turn loose of my wife, Penrose," Quinn growled, very much on his mock dignity, "or she will wrinkle your cravat past all bearing."

"For the pleasure of properly greeting Her Grace, I will endure even that tribulation." Joshua kissed Jane's cheek with a hint of his old insouciance.

Only a hint. Jane allowed herself to cling for one more precious minute, but it would take days at least to regain her composure where Joshua Penrose was concerned.

He was back, but was he *home*? Jane could not be sure. He was almost gaunt, quieter in his movements and speech, but also more real, more present. One no longer had the sense that the handsome Mr. Penrose was exuding effortless charm as much for his own amusement as from a sense of bred-in social duty.

"I would in the normal course ring for tea," Jane said, "but the situation calls for something more celebratory. Ned is fond of champagne punch. Will that do?"

The men—Quinn, Joshua, and Ned, lurking by the porter's nook—exchanged glances. *Her Grace is to be indulged in all matters,* which saved Jane the trouble of managing any of her menfolk into submission.

"Punch will suit splendidly," Joshua said, undoing the buttons of a modestly stylish greatcoat. Three capes, fashionable without being flamboyant. He wore no scarf when the old Joshua would have sported about in some tastefully colorful silk creation. He hung his hat on a hook, bowed to Quinn, and then extended a hand. "Your Grace, greetings."

Quinn astonished the stuffing out of Jane by pulling Joshua into a hug, thumping him on the back, and enduring a thump in return.

Because Jane was standing near the front door, she could see Joshua's face reflected in the mirror over the sideboard. His expression went from surprise to pleasure to something too vulnerable to look upon. Vast, enormous relief, certainly, but also...

As Quinn delivered the *coup de bienvenue*, or whatever men called it, Jane put a name to that fleeting light in Joshua's eyes.

This effusive welcome was *unnerving* him. Threatening his composure, touching his heart.

"About damned time you wandered home," Quinn said. "The bank is on the brink of failure, my siblings have driven me halfway to Bedlam, the monarchy is in the hands of a man by turns shrewd and silly, and I have had no partner on hand to help me manage any of it. Poor Jane despairs of my tirades. Not well done of you, Penrose."

"I have braved the North Atlantic twice," Joshua replied, stepping back. "Endured the company of a lot of thieving barbarians, made the bank considerable coin, and had to content myself with mere dispatches masquerading as ducal correspondence. It's about time you gave me a proper report instead of a lot of gossip and whinging."

They bared their teeth at each other while Ned pretended to study the chandelier. Jane had hung a fresh kissing bough in the foyer a mere day ago, though not a single white berry remained on the sprigs of mistletoe.

"Into the family parlor, gentlemen," she said. "We must have some treats to celebrate your return, lest Cook go into a decline. She has been baking Joshua's favorite anise stars in anticipation of welcoming the prodigal banker, and we must not upset her in the middle of the holiday season."

For some reason, this announcement inspired a guffaw out of Ned, a snicker from the duke, and soft laughter from Joshua.

That laughter warmed Jane's heart as nothing else could have. Joshua might be too thin, too serious, and acting a bit oddly, but he was home, he was giving as good as he got, and his humor was genuine.

Whatever sorrows had befallen him, he would come right in time and was already well on the way.

Jane sat through Quinn's recounting of each sibling's current situation, and when talk turned to banking affairs, she rose.

"I lack the fortitude to withstand business talk on Boxing Day. I will repel boarders in the formal parlor while you gentlemen plot the salvation of the realm's financial future."

Joshua rose and bowed. "Your Grace, a pleasure to see you again, even if you are keeping dubious company these days. I will not be a stranger in future. You have my word on that. I apologize for being so laggardly in coming to call. I needed time to recover from my travels before I felt presentable."

Jane had needed to hear those words, and he'd known it. However brief Joshua's marriage had been, he'd learned from it.

"See that you make a regular nuisance of yourself, sir," Jane said. "Or I will make a nuisance of myself, and that thought should give you nightmares. Don't spoil your luncheon, gentlemen."

"Right," Ned said, rising as well. "Cook's nerves and all that. I will join Her Grace on the figurative parapets or the poop deck, whatever the metaphor ought to be. Penrose, welcome home."

Jane made it as far as the corridor before she turned into Ned's gentle embrace and had herself a nice little weep, without which no family holiday would be complete. She dispatched Ned to hang fresh mistletoe in the foyer and spared him for the present from giving his latest report.

Though Jane did wonder when recovering from travels had started to require keeping company with a pretty widow and her half-grown daughter?

"Your visit went well," Hope said, twining her arm through Joshua's. "The visit you made this morning to your friends." As opposed to the several calls he'd made with Hope and Holly that afternoon. They were strolling home from Mrs. Colchester's. That lady had declared herself the original camellia enthusiast and asked for cuttings from the more vivid bushes.

So cheerful at this dreary time of year, you know. Hope had found the comment telling, given that the sun was beaming brilliantly on piles of snow, and icicles sparkled from every eave.

"Mrs. Colchester needs a cat to cheer her up," Holly said. "When I play with Heifer, I laugh because he's so silly. I shall tell Heifer all about Mrs. Colchester's porcelain figures."

A beautiful white crèche, complete with ox, ass, camel, and lamb, done so delicately that the creatures appeared to regard the baby with contented fondness. No cat, though, which even Mrs. Colchester had allowed was a curious omission in a stable.

Holly ran ahead, pausing only to exchange a few words with Slivers, who was doing a spanking business tidying the intersection nearest the house.

"My call did go well," Joshua said. "My friends were pleased to see me, I was pleased to see them, and... I'm making the whole encounter sound mundane and even a little tedious when, in truth, words are inadequate for the occasion. My friends were worried."

Hope finished with the important part. "Worried *about you.*"

He nodded. "Very. And they didn't care that I meandered on the way to their door, didn't care that I hadn't sent word from the docks.

They simply wanted me safe. I don't believe I have ever been the personification of answered prayers before."

"Yes, you have."

A little hitch of surprise in Joshua's gait communicated itself to Hope. "You aren't teasing?"

"Nor am I flirting in the present moment, though there are prayers and there are *prayers*. When you toddled along this very street with that first sack of provisions, you answered every prayer my belly had been uttering for days and nights." More to the point, he'd doubtless answered Holly's prayers and a few of Heifer's too.

"You answered a prayer or two of mine as well, Hope."

He wasn't flirting either. "Go on." What could she have possibly…?

"You did not have to allow me to stay that first night. Had you ordered me out into the storm, I would have gone."

"I know, which is partly why I didn't. I did not trust that you'd find your way to the Wood and Willow."

"I might not have."

Quite an admission. Quite a sad admission. "Because at least in death you might be with your Maureen and Eric? You must know that, for thinking that way, both Maureen's and Eric's ghosts would scold you mightily."

"As I reproach myself, but you don't scold, and you do understand. That makes such a difference."

"Storms pass. Recalling that might help the next time your thinking grows muddled." That they could discuss Maureen, Eric, Edwin, Orson, or Alma might have struck Hope as odd a few days ago. Now, that openness was one more lovely aspect of time spent with Joshua.

And need not be belabored.

"Tell me more about your friends," Hope said as they turned onto their street. "What was in the package you left in the larder?"

"Jane and Quinn's cook sent me home with enough sweets and treats to give every boy in the conservatory the king of all bellyaches.

We will have to ration the abundance. I have a semi-aversion to anise, so I developed the habit of taking an anise star from the holiday treat tray first, to blunt my appetite. The myth has arisen in certain quarters that they are my favorite. I dearly hope the boys can appreciate them, because I cannot."

"I like them. My favorite will always be warm gingerbread with plenty of butter." Preferably shared with Joshua.

That thought dimmed some of the day's sparkle.

"Fresh gingerbread is high on my list as well," Joshua said. "I'd like you to meet Their Graces."

"Who?"

"Their Graces, my friends, Quinn and Jane. They have the honor—the dubious honor in Quinn's opinion—to be the Duke and Duchess of Walden."

Hope stopped in the middle of the walkway. "You are *friends* with a duke and duchess?"

"The friendship predates the title, at least with Quinn and me. He was a brash, canny Yorkshireman trying to establish himself in banking circles here in London. He went about it all wrong, and I told him so. He invited me outside, and I feared he meant to try conclusions with me in the stable yard. I would not have emerged victorious from such an encounter with Quinn, if I emerged at all."

A large icicle on the house across the street dropped and shattered, spooking a passing horse.

"You are friends with a duke who tried to *brawl* with you?"

Joshua smiled. "He asked me what suggestions I had for improving his approach. My first suggestion was to find an elocution teacher. My second bit of advice was to focus on the customers nobody else took much interest in. The smaller shopkeepers who might invest in a silver service in lieu of stashing money in a bank. He heeded my advice, and that led eventually to a partnership."

"Widows," Hope said, resuming her progress. "This is the Wentworth and Penrose bank, and you are *the* Penrose. Every widow I know advises me to entrust my assets to Wentworth's." Though, until the house sold, there would not be any assets.

"I am the present Penrose." Joshua ambled along beside her, apparently knowing better than to offer his arm. "My grandfather was the original article, but my uncles bungled his legacy."

"What of your father?"

"I barely recall him, though I'm said to resemble him closely. Big, hearty, doted on Mama. He was knocked into eternity in a coaching accident."

Hope was not angry, exactly, but she was flustered. "And your mother?"

"Grandpapa looked after her and me, though the financial business eventually passed into my uncles' hands. Repairing the damage they did took some time, and in that regard, Quinn Wentworth, as he was styled at the time, had some excellent investment strategies."

Meaning Joshua's mama had been a widow cast upon the charity of family. "Your bank looks after widows."

"We look after all of our customers. His Grace is particularly adept at seeing that bereaved women and, in some cases, bereaved men are not taken advantage of. His Grace has no patience with predatory greed." Joshua walked along in silence until they reached the front steps of the house.

Hope's house.

"Quinn was raised not simply in poverty, Hope, but in abject squalor. His mother succumbed before Quinn was grown, the father not much later, and I gather that was for the best. Quinn doesn't talk about it. His siblings nevertheless told me enough that I know he and they have overcome unimaginable odds. He was convicted of a murder he did not commit... He and Jane were married in Newgate, of all places. They are remarkable people."

Joshua's voice conveyed the next thing to awe, which made Hope want to shake him.

"*You* are remarkable. You gave this brawling, ill-bred, overgrown orphan a chance before Society had to give him the time of day. You put your faith in him and apparently stood by him through all of his tribulations, which frankly sound to me like something from a Gothic novel. Of course, the Wentworths were unnerved by your departure. You were the answer to their prayers, you daft man."

Joshua peered around the slushy, sunny, bustling street. "Are you angry?"

"I don't know what I am, but we'd best get along and make sure Holly is not investigating the treats in the pantry."

Joshua winged his arm, his expression unreadable. Hope took it and allowed him to escort her up the steps.

She knew what the roiling in her gut was, knew what that irritable, anxious edge to her voice meant. She was *afraid*.

Joshua was not only friends with a duke, he'd been a sort of guardian angel to the man. Joshua of snow-shoveling fame was also respected in Mayfair and the City, having turned around an ailing bank, then expanded it to the New World apparently.

And successfully so.

By the time Hope was passing Joshua her bonnet, her new gloves folded into the crown, some calm had returned.

"I should have suspected you are rich," Hope said. "This is a very fine house, and you occupied it prior to your travels."

"I was literally penniless when I turned up on your doorstep, Hope. I simply like good art."

"And old desks, and fine carpets, and elegant clocks—Edwin loved your clocks—and if you will excuse me, I'd better locate Holly."

"She is in the conservatory considering which bushes will make the best cuttings for Mrs. Colchester."

Without even cocking an ear, Hope knew Joshua was right. "I need time to consider, Joshua. I am not angry, but I am having to adjust my thinking, and widowhood has made me wary of that exercise when it is forced upon me."

"I understand, but allow me to impart an idea or two before you embark on these adjustments, hmm?"

He did understand Hope's need to ponder the day's revelations.

Of course he would. Loss had a way of casting a pall over any change, even positive changes.

"I'm listening."

He took her hand and led her to the parlor, then set about building up the fire. The room was cozy, tidy, and now full of memories that would have put Hope to the blush were they not so precious.

"Their Grace's cook is a formidable lady. She is ferociously loyal to the family and they to her. She can cook the fancy dishes and supervise the mandatory formal dinners, but she prides herself on knowing each person's favorite desserts and so forth, whether that's raspberry fool, cheese toast, or some fancy French creation. She considers me family."

Hope settled in the wing chair rather than risk the sofa. "And?"

"I braved her purlieus to thank her for the sweets and to allow a parade inspection of my prodigal person belowstairs. I also wanted to leave as unobtrusively as possible. The first things I spotted were three of Edwin's toasting racks, and when I asked Cook about them, she said no proper kitchen is without at least one. She also has three of his apple-coring devices and showed me a pair of gloves that are made of oilskin—"

"—roughened on the palms with some sort of ceramic paste," Hope said, "that makes scrubbing carrots and potatoes quick and easy. I scrubbed the skin right off many a potato with mine before they wore out. But I thought..."

Joshua perched on the hassock. "You thought Edwin's patents went nowhere? A ducal kitchen is quite somewhere for clever inventions of that nature, Hope. Cook is very proud to have the latest in labor-saving inventions among her arsenal."

A very competent, ducal cook. One on nodding terms at market with her peers and doubtless happy to chat endlessly with them about the tools of her trade.

Three toasting racks.

Three apple corers.

Even the scrubbing gloves. Edward had had high hopes for those gloves. Much safer for scullery maids and potboys than wielding a knife.

Hope stared at the cheerful blaze on the hearth, mind awhirl. "I... see."

Joshua positioned himself knee to knee with her and took her hand in his. "What do you see?"

A lot of questions, not enough answers. "We shall pay a call on Mr. Peters tomorrow, if you are willing."

"Of course I am willing. You don't want to wait until the New Year?"

"I don't think I can bear to."

"Then tomorrow it is."

Hope grabbed him in a hug, then rose. "Let's save the camellias, shall we? Sufficient unto the day and all that."

She sailed out of the parlor before Joshua could demand more discussion. Cowardly of her, like Edwin going for his walks to the pub when Holly had been cranky, but the holidays thus far had been one adjustment after another.

Providence alone knew what additional adjustments might be demanded of Hope come the New Year. Sufficient unto the day indeed.

Sufficient unto the holiday, more like.

CHAPTER TEN

More temperate weather had turned the streets and walkways muddy, which was probably why Hope had assented to Joshua commandeering the bank's coach and four for the excursion to Peters's office.

She wasn't saying much, and she hadn't intruded on Joshua's slumbers in the parlor the night before. She would have taken easily to the taciturn, hulking Yorkshireman Quinn had been years ago. Now, she clearly did not like that Joshua was *that* Penrose, or that he was wealthy, or that his business partner was a duke.

She cared not at all for such surprises, and Joshua positively loathed that his situation upset her.

"I'm nervous," Hope said as the coach swayed around a corner. "I should not be."

I'm nervous too, though for different reasons. "Peters works for you, Hope. He worked for Edwin, or led Edwin to believe that was the arrangement. Do you recall how they met?"

"Something to do with filing patents, I believe, and Edwin mentioned to Peters that he wanted us settled in a proper London house. Peters had a perfect property on offer for a client. I suspect

Edwin had already begun to feel ill, but he wasn't admitting it to himself, much less to me."

Did Hope suspect she'd been swindled? "I am very good with money and figures," Joshua said slowly. "I don't have to work at it. I understand what a ledger is saying without having to decipher the information line by line. The numbers speak to me."

Hope sent him a sidewise glance. "And?"

"I am useless when it comes to sketching and drawing. My trees look like mushrooms. My horses like some sort of sheep-cow hybrid without horns. This is part of the reason I enjoy good art so much."

The coach slowed to a crawl.

"You're saying Edwin could not be a genius at everything. I know that, but he never let me manage anything more than my pin money. Had an old-fashioned view of domestic finances, though one doesn't learn such things about a spouse until after the vows are spoken."

I want to marry you. Another rejoinder best kept for another time, assuming—as Joshua had been—that Hope was even open to the notion of remarrying.

"If I were in your shoes, Hope, I would be furious."

"Furious with myself because I have been duped over the patent income?"

If Joshua's suspicions were correct, she'd been duped in many regards. "Furious with Peters, who has done the duping. He's a crook, and he thinks he's been successful stealing the last groat you and Holly have."

"The Christmas basket was very tasteful." Said with an encouraging degree of asperity.

The Christmas basket had been an insult. "He has stolen from *Holly,* and he preyed on a dying man to set up crooked schemes. If I were Peters, I'd be in the next thing to a panic. I'd be living in terror of the day when Hope Burdette got wise to my plundering and came looking for retribution."

"I have never terrified anybody in all my born days, Joshua Penrose."

"I can't say I've accomplished much beyond a timely and well-deserved intimidation or two, but I've seen Quinn frighten grown men nigh into incontinence. He never raises his voice, he never answers questions—he asks the questions—and he allows innuendo to do the work of threats. All three tactics are available to you. You probably use them with Holly to very good effect."

Hope sat up a little straighter. "I want to speak for myself. I know that much."

"You ask the questions. You very civilly demand the answers. I thought the Christmas basket was a little understated, myself, but I do wonder if it wasn't charged to your account."

Hope's brows rose. "More stealing under the guise of generous consideration. Speaking softly might be beyond me."

"Then I pray the clerks have opened the windows so that all of London will hear you putting Peters in his place."

She raised the shade on her side of the coach. "His place is Newgate, or perdition, if my suspicions are correct. He did steal from Holly. He did take advantage of poor Edwin."

"Now he's dealing with *you.* I would pity the man, but he deserves to be held accountable. If he's preying upon your family, Hope, he's likely cheating other clients out of their life savings as well."

The effect of that surmise was lovely. The Widow Burdette gathered up her reticule, gloves, and muff. As she assembled her accessories, she similarly collected both implacable dignity and unshakable resolve. She'd dressed in the dove gray of second mourning for this outing and completed her preparations by lowering the black net veil pinned to her bonnet brim.

As a knight might lower a visor prior to galloping into the lists.

"You are my prospective banker?" she asked in a clipped, businesslike tone.

"I have that pleasure if you say so." Joshua would rather be her fiancé, but to be her banker for the next hour was an honor in itself.

The coach came to a halt outside a row of handsome three-story houses. Save for a pub on the corner, the street boasted not a single shop. The walkways were shoveled and the porch lamps sparkling.

Here, discreet, prosperous business was done, or so the appearances suggested.

"I'm angry," Joshua said, meaning it. "I'm angry on your behalf, but a crook in the countinghouse also gives all who handle money honestly a harder job. When you take Peters to task, you strike a blow for all honest people in trade too, Hope."

She nodded. "I shall be a fire-breathing dragon who does not raise her voice, does not tolerate questions, and allows innuendo to do the work of threats. Any mama or governess worth her salt can accomplish that much before breakfast."

Peters would not know what hit him, but if he was smart, he'd know to stay down and protect his head, for the drubbing would be very, very thorough.

~

Mr. Peters wasn't in, and the relief Hope felt at that news shamed her. She wanted to put the confrontation off, not because holding a scoundrel to account was hard, but because a small, timid part of her wanted to be wrong.

Mr. Peters was *not* a scoundrel.

He had *not* cheated Edwin out of a sizable sum.

He would *never* be so dastardly as to enjoy the revenue that Edwin's creativity and hard work had earned.

The quality of Joshua's silence in the coach had warned Hope otherwise. There was more to Peters's scheming than Joshua had said, but stealing the patent revenue was bad enough.

"When might Mr. Peters be expected back?" Hope asked the genial Mr. Plodgely.

A crash sounded from behind a closed door. Plodgely's smile faltered. "Beg pardon, Mrs. Burdette, Mr., um, sir. I brought my sons with me today—Mama and daughter were off to the shops—and the boys can be a bit rambunctious."

He bowed and withdrew, leaving Hope and Joshua among a half-dozen clerks at their high tables, none of whom was willing to so much as glance at Hope.

A man's voice, raised in ire came from behind the door, and Mr. Plodgely returned holding several large pieces of what might have once been a ceramic vase.

"Beg pardon," he said again. "Mr. Peters isn't expected back until after the New Year. We all agree he's earned himself a nice long holiday."

One of the clerks raised his head, then checked himself and went back to his copying.

"No matter," Hope said. "My questions were not urgent." But now that she'd arrived unannounced, Peters would be on his guard. Drat and blast.

"Perhaps you might answer a few questions for Mrs. Burdette?" Joshua asked, all diffidence and masculine patience.

Plodgely drew himself up. "I am always happy to be of service to our clients."

"You there," Hope said, addressing the clerk who'd almost looked up. "Tend to the boys and set them to working sums or copying or something useful. They are bored witless and have had too many sweets for days on end, none of which is their fault."

The hapless fellow looked from her to Plodgely, who appeared to have lost his grasp of plain English.

Hope clapped her gloved hands at the clerk. "Be off with you, or they'll smash Mr. Peters's bust of Blackstone next, and heaven knows where the funds for a replacement might come from."

The man got off his backside and shepherded the boys into some sort of conference room while Plodgely gaped.

Joshua was right. One did not have to raise one's voice or make explicit threats.

"My office is through here," Plodgely said. "Would anybody care for tea?"

Hope was not about to be distracted with who took his with sugar and who preferred milk.

"None for me, and I daresay my banker doesn't care for any either." The moment had not yet arrived to introduce Joshua by name.

Plodgely ushered them into a space where evidence of industry did battle with the forces of tidiness and order. Briefs tied up in red ribbons were scattered on a long table by the window. Law books were open on the desk, the table, and windowsills, and an abacus lay on its side on the desk blotter.

A standing desk by the window held yet more law books, three opened and layered atop each other. The room had no less than four inkwells, and another abacus sat on the mantel. A map of the Thames hung above the fireplace, and a portrait of King George held pride of place opposite the desk.

No sketches of the children, no holiday touches. The shine on the elbows of Mr. Plodgely's morning coat and the worn heels on his shoes suggested that a lack of coin figured in his decorative choices.

"Now, then," he said, moving books into stacks on the table. "What can I do for you, Mrs. Burdette?"

The wording Hope had decided on was simple. "I'd like to see the accounting of my patent revenues." Hers, willed to her by Edwin, who had been a genius at inventing useful gadgets.

Plodgely ceased heaving tomes into piles. "For the year? We haven't done the year-end totals yet, ma'am. I can show you the detailed ledger for this year, and we certainly have last year's totals done."

"I'd like to see both." That he'd accede to her request so easily astonished Hope and made her bold. "I'd also like to see my payment balance as it compares to the mortgage sum still owing."

"I might have to dig a bit for that. As you know, Mr. Peters handled your accounts personally."

"Sooner begun is sooner done," Hope replied sweetly while Joshua pretended to absorb himself with the view of the street below.

"Quite right, ma'am. Mrs. Plodgely reminds me of the same frequently." He went to his shelves, extracted a volume bound in green leather, and passed it to Hope. "Patent revenues from inception to date, in chronological order. Mr. Burdette's talents were substantial."

On that note, he decamped.

"Either Plodgely is the best actor ever to avoid Drury Lane," Joshua said, "or he's a complete dupe."

Hope set her reticule atop the law books on the standing desk, and Joshua held a chair for her at the head of the table.

"How can you tell?"

"I offer only a guess based on observation." Joshua took the chair to her right. "If Plodgely knew Peters was stealing from you, and Peters had any indication that his scheme had been detected, Peters would pay Plodgely enough to keep silent. I grant you, raising three children takes coin, but a solicitor who cannot afford new heels or a clean blotter is in straitened circumstances."

"My thought as well." Though she hadn't noticed the blotter. "He needs a new jacket too."

Joshua nodded at the ledger. "Let's have a look, shall we?"

Five minutes later, with Joshua on hand to confirm the significance of the numbers, Hope was in shock.

"All this money. All this money earned by Edwin's inventions, and I've seen not a penny of it. I've *paid* Peters... He said any patent revenue, however small, would go toward paying off the mortgage at the time of sale."

Joshua extracted from his tail pocket a little book of bound blank pages such as an artist would keep handy. He penciled figures in a rapid, tidy hand.

"I suspect," he said as he wrote, "there is no mortgage. Peters doubtless created a document for Edwin to sign that looks like some sort of loan agreement, and the word 'mortgage' might appear in the language somewhere, but it's a complete work of fiction."

"A work of fraud, you mean, while my life for the past two and a half years has been very nearly a tragedy, Joshua. Peters can be hanged for this, can't he?"

"Transported, possibly, but the crown's chief witness, your late husband, is not available to testify. Proof becomes an issue, though not an insurmountable one."

If anybody knew how to address that issue, Joshua did. That he was Hope's banker of the moment gave her inordinate comfort.

"I don't want him to hang, Joshua. I want him to pay."

"He shall."

Plodgely bustled back in, a slim red volume in his hands. "I found it! Up to date and in Mr. Peters's own hand. Every penny of the mortgage payments." He passed Hope the ledger and hovered like a schoolboy awaiting praise.

Hope scanned the last page, recalling fingers aching with too many hours of fine stitching, a mind clouded with endless worry, Holly sighing at the empty larder and promising Heifer a lick of butter when next they had any.

"And what is the unpaid mortgage balance?" she asked, passing the ledger to Joshua before she yielded to the impulse to heave it through the window.

"Beg pardon? The unpaid balance?"

"The amount still owing on the loan secured by the house where I now dwell," Hope said, keeping her voice level with effort. "My late husband paid a substantial sum to complete the sale of the premises, and I was made aware of the mortgage only after Mr. Burdette's passing. What is the outstanding principal still owing?"

Plodgely gazed out the window. He rocked up and down on his worn heels. He considered the portrait of Mad George on the far wall.

"I do not know why Mr. Peters hasn't listed a running account of the mortgage balance," Plodgely said. "The figure is of concern to most clients and certainly to any lenders."

"As to that," Joshua said, closing the book with a snap, "who is the lender? Who holds Mrs. Burdette's mortgage?"

Plodgely smiled. "That's a simple explanation, sir. Mrs. Burdette's house is the former residence of the banker Mr. Joshua Penrose, who sold the property through intermediaries some years after he decamped for the colonies. Mr. Penrose was moved by Mr. Burdette's situation, according to Mr. Peters, and offered to hold the mortgage personally rather than through his bank. This has allowed Mr. Peters some discretion in the area of late payments and such."

He beamed at them with all the goodwill of the season and then some.

"How generous of Mr. Penrose," Joshua muttered, rising. "We'd still like to know the amount owing."

"I can do the calculations," Plodgely said. "I simply need to find the mortgage document, which will tell us the interest rate, the initial sum establishing the borrower's equity, and other relevant terms."

"Five percent per annum," Hope said, "according to Mr. Peters. Mr. Penrose wasn't really all that generous, was he?"

Plodgely's good humor faded. "That doesn't make sense. If the interest is that high, and you have all this revenue... I don't understand why you haven't been given an opportunity to purchase the house outright, unless there's a non-acceleration clause. Those are very dirty tactics, and I cannot imagine Mr. Peters allowing any client of ours to agree to such language."

Hope should have boxed Plodgely's ears or launched a tirade at him for his gullibility. Instead, his earnest acceptance of the situation at face value was reassuring.

A solicitor, a man who transacted business every day and who was the support of three children and a wife, hadn't detected Peters's schemes when they were hatched beneath his very nose.

"Mr. Penrose," Hope said, "would you explain the situation to Mr. Plodgely as succinctly as possible? I would like to make the acquaintance of his children. I'm sure they are darling boys, and I have seen enough figures for one day."

Joshua bowed. "Of course, ma'am. This shouldn't take long."

Hope left as Plodgely sank into the chair by the window. "Beg pardon, sir, but did Mrs. Burdette say your name was... *Penrose*?"

CHAPTER ELEVEN

"Mr. Plodgely will keep mum?" Hope asked, folding her veil back up over her hat brim. She extracted a pin from the crown of her bonnet, a long, dangerous-looking item tipped with jet. The gleaming hatpin echoed some sentiment gleaming just as brightly in her eyes.

Triumph, glee—Joshua wasn't sure what, but she fairly sparkled with it.

"Allow me." He carefully plucked the pin from her hand. "In a moving coach, you could put your eye out with this thing." He arranged the veil atop the brim and sat back.

He wanted to take Hope's hand, but he also wanted to allow her a moment to bask in her success. In her newfound wealth *and* her success.

"Plodgely will go home," Joshua said, "have a very frank talk with his missus, and conclude that his best course is to plead ignorance, which he can honestly do. He will remind all and sundry that when it came to your accounts, and that of several other bereaved clients, Mr. Peters managed the finances personally."

"Several others?"

"Plodgely mentioned four off the top of his head. He's not stupid.

He simply lacks guile." Which was very likely why Peters had kept him on. "He works hard, he's honest, the clerks like him, though I'd bet you a shilling they refer to him as Beg Pardon behind his back." Clerks and schoolboys enjoyed many of the same pastimes.

"Plodgely's sons are very nice little fellows," Hope said. "We must ensure Peters's crimes do not redound upon the innocent."

Joshua still did not venture to take Hope's hand. Something about her tone—a bit distracted, a little distant—prevented him.

"Plodgely and I discussed next steps," Joshua said. "He will examine the relevant client ledgers in Peters's absence and will, when the moment is right, inform those clients that the market has improved where their investments are concerned. He also hinted that Peters's personal bankbook sits in the firm's safe and that a discreet inspection of same might occur after all the clerks have left early."

Hope stared hard at the empty bench opposite. "Peters must pay, Joshua. I want the money coming out of *his* pocket, and in its place, I want him carrying around worry for how he'll eat, where he'll live, and whether he will have an old age to fret over."

"Would you also like him paying five percent interest on the sums stolen?"

Some of her distraction faded. "Oh, yes. Interest. Interest would be lovely."

Joshua took the length of the next street to consider what further measures might effect justice in Hope's eyes. "Do you wish for Peters to sell his share of the firm to Plodgely for one pound?"

Hope's eyes took on a warmth an entire loaf of fresh, buttery gingerbread might have inspired. "I would like that very much, and might it be arranged that Peters announces a hasty decision to retire? A notice in *The Times* to that effect, on the financial pages and in whatever periodicals the solicitors read."

Well, of course. Take away his livelihood, just as he'd taken away Hope's access to all of Edwin's earnings and to that good man's savings.

"When the alternative is ruin and transportation, I'm sure Peters will accept the need to quit his practice."

If Peters were smart, he had some means stashed out of sight, unknown to his employees, neighbors, or family, if any family he had. He would need every penny of his reserves just to survive by the time Joshua was done carrying out Hope's orders.

"I am proud of you," Joshua said. "You handled the situation quite well." Like a lady who solved more pressing challenges every day before noon.

"Proud of me." Hope patted his knee. "I am proud of me too. I daresay Edwin, strutting around in his wings and halo, is proud of me as well. He did not fail me, Joshua, not as I'd feared he had. He was simply too trusting, and so was I. Might we stop at a bakery?"

"Of course, but we should also stop at my bank."

"Because my funds will be moved there. Yes, of course. But the bakery first, Joshua. Transacting business has left me peckish, and I can afford fresh gingerbread now."

She could afford to buy the whole bakery, as well as a herd of ponies for Holly and a cheesemonger's shop for Heifer.

"What will you do with your funds, Hope?"

She gave his knee a final, slow caress. "I don't know. Buy a house, I suppose. There never was a mortgage, was there?"

"Plodgely never saw a bill of sale, never saw a loan agreement, and confirmed that as far as he knew, his firm has never had dealings with Chumley, who handles my personal affairs. We can safely assume Edwin did not buy the house."

My house, though thinking of it thus brought no joy. The opposite, in fact.

"Just as well. The place is too big, exorbitantly expensive to heat, and full of all manner of appointments too fine for my tastes. Edwin would have it, though, and I thought perhaps a famous inventor needed an imposing domicile. He planned to turn the conservatory into his shop."

The very idea should have made Joshua shudder, but heating the whole vast space just to keep plants warm certainly qualified as a vanity. Edwin's inventions made life easier and safer for many. That the conservatory now housed a surreptitious complement of discarded boys was somehow fitting.

"You don't need to make any decisions at the moment," Joshua said. "That house is Holly's home, and she need not leave it until you are ready to make a change."

She need not leave it at all, if Joshua could persuade Hope to marry him, but the longer the coach rattled along the Strand and the longer the reality of Hope's changed circumstances settled into Joshua's mind—Edwin's inventions were quite lucrative and would be for years—the less confident he was that the New Year would see a proper courtship begun.

Joshua directed the coachman to stop at the bakery patronized by the bank, and rather than send the footman to secure the coveted treat, he escorted Hope inside.

"That aroma, that fragrance of baking treats, must be the scent of heaven," Hope said, perusing a glass-topped case full of artfully displayed French confections. "These are too pretty to eat."

"Made fresh this mornin'," the plump lady behind the counter said, "and they taste even better than they look. I know a certain duchess who favors the chocolate tarts, and they are scrumptious, if I do say so my own self."

She wore a pristine cap and full-length apron, and her countenance would have been appropriate for Father Christmas's wife. The shop bell tinkled merrily, and the windows were festooned with greenery, though Joshua was feeling anything but cheerful.

As Hope deliberated over a boxful of assorted treats, Joshua saw her slipping off into a new, secure, happy life without him. No financial exigencies or confusion about house ownership would throw them together, and he'd be relegated to meeting with her quarterly to review accounts—or worse, with her solicitor—until she decided to move her funds to another bank.

Then, one day, he'd see a small announcement in the Society pages, and…

"What's your favorite?" Hope asked. "I know you do not care for the anise biscuits, and you can do full justice to your half of any slice of gingerbread, but which one is your favorite?"

You. You are my favorite, with your determination and pragmatism, and disdain for vanities, and your devotion to your child and to that stupid cat.

Who was, in fact, a sage among felines.

"Mr. Penrose adores Italian cream cake," the lady behind the counter said. "I do recognize you, sir, though you could use some good tucker, and I've probably put on a few pounds since you sailed all those years ago. You were a very loyal client, or so you'd have us believe."

She put a slice of pale, rich cake into the box, managing not to touch any of the treasures already arranged therein.

"He sneaked half the goods to those naughty boys that bank employs," the lady went on. "They aren't so naughty after the bank gets hold of them, though, and some of them aren't boys anymore. Will there be anything else?"

"Another box," Joshua said. "For the bank's boys." Hope had already ordered enough for the conservatory lodgers to feast on until Twelfth Night.

The footman was summoned to collect the boxes, and Joshua escorted Hope back out to the waiting coach and four.

She assumed the forward-facing bench, the boxes on the seat opposite. Joshua resumed his place beside her, a privilege he might soon lose.

"I fear," Hope said, "that I will wake up, be once again a pauper, and find all those delicacies are hallucinations born of prolonged hunger."

"The delicacies are real." Had the attraction between them been real? Joshua could answer in the affirmative for himself, unequivocally.

"You are thinking of Mr. Peters, aren't you?" Hope asked. "I never want to see him again, Joshua. The thought of him infuriates me, and I might well do him an injury if I lay eyes on him."

"I will summon him to the bank, ask His Grace and Mr. Edward Wentworth to join the meeting as my witnesses, and see your wishes regarding Peters's fate carried out. He will doubtless leave London posthaste for more affordable climes where English law does not pertain."

Paris, perhaps, or Scotland. Scottish winters were not to be trifled with.

"You are all business, Joshua. I can see why your bank prospered. I would hardly associate the man who hung paper stars for Holly with the stern, imposing figure who turned Plodgely's knees weak. You make quite an impression."

"I've been around finance since I was not much older than Holly. Grandpapa insisted that handling other people's money was as sacred a trust as handling their health, their offspring, or their confidences. Peters has much to answer for."

Hope eyed the boxes on the opposite bench. "Will our business at the bank take long?"

She was still Hope. Still the self-possessed, sensible lady he adored. No treats in a moving coach, lest something spill.

"Our business won't take long at all. The documents were prepared in advance at my direction." He led Hope through the bank's front doors.

Because the days between Christmas and the New Year were a period of intense commercial activity, they found the bank lobby, usually a quiet, airy space, thronged. Customers stood before every teller's window. More stood in small groups chatting, and others enjoyed servings of mulled cider from a punchbowl attended by a liveried footman beneath the rotunda skylight.

"This is very grand," Hope said, voice lowered. "Like a museum or even a palace."

Joshua paused to let her take in the splendor of the lobby, which had been built mostly to his specifications.

"We wanted abundant light and plenty of space. Customers should enjoy coming here and being seen here." Joshua hadn't missed the place, exactly, but it did show to good advantage with a few tasteful wreaths on the balcony rails and a pretty red ribbon threaded along the carved bannisters.

As they stood, taking in the scene, the conversational hum ebbed, and Joshua realized that the tellers were no longer transacting business. All eyes had turned to him and Hope, standing by the door.

A tall, exquisitely attired figure advanced along the balcony.

"Who is that man?" Hope whispered. "He'd look like the Wrath of the City, except for that little boutonniere on his lapel."

"My partner," Joshua whispered back. "His Grace excels at exuding consequence." Quinn was looking exceedingly dignified, as only Quinn could, even amid holiday trappings and customers slightly tipsy on the bank's punch.

"Mr. Penrose." Quinn had adopted ducal tones, his voice filling the now-quiet bank. "Welcome back at long last. Your return is the best holiday gift that I or this bank could have asked for. *You were much missed.*"

Joshua endured the chorus of *welcome back, sirs* and the hip-hip-hooray that coalesced from them. Hope stood beside him, making he knew not what of the greetings.

"Come along," Joshua said when conversation had resumed at a considerably higher pitch, and people were raising glasses and beaming in his direction. "I'll introduce you."

"To the duke?"

"To the duke, whom I occasionally refer to as Wentworth, though that's no longer proper address. He's just a man, Hope, and rather shy, especially when he hasn't his duchess on hand. He's a very good banker, though, and an excellent friend."

If one didn't mind the company of a ducal porcupine on occasion or little welcome-home fetes conducted before half of Mayfair, with the prodigal all unaware of his impending honors.

They got through the introductions mostly because Ned took on the role of host, served the cider, and kept the paperwork moving all without appearing to transact any business at all. Quinn, of course, exhorted Joshua to bring Mrs. Burdette around to meet the duchess, which caused Hope to blush and Joshua to think longingly of weeks on the high seas.

Not how he'd seen the day going, though this was very close to the planned version of events and proof of the most successful outcome possible for Hope.

"You are quiet," Hope said when they were again in the coach. "That was quite some welcome, Mr. Penrose."

Don't Mr. Penrose me now. "Quinn has a good sense of how to handle the appearances. He did not want me sneaking up the bank's back steps, the bitter widower who cannot be bothered to greet clerks and tellers he's known for years. I suspected there'd be some sort of fuss, but not that."

Not in front of Hope, for pity's sake.

"If that was a mere fuss, I shudder to consider what your welcome-home ball will entail."

"As do I, so please don't mention the notion." He'd spoken with less humor and more asperity than he'd intended, but Jane was entirely capable of pulling exactly that sort of stunt.

Joshua was on the point of extracting a promise from Hope that she'd attend any ensuing balls with him, as his devoted escort and bodyguard, when the coach drew up in front of the house.

"Holly has apparently recruited more urchins," Hope said as the footman let down the steps. "I don't recognize them."

Several children were on the front terrace, and they were not attired as urchins. Three girls counting Holly and two boys.

"Those," Joshua said, "might be what is referred to as playmates." Holly was waving madly, and somebody had ensured she was properly bundled up.

Snow adorned the clothing of two of the children, attesting to a battle fought to completion. Smiles all around confirmed that neither side had suffered any grievous wounds. The girl on the end had the same red hair Holly did, and that realization left Joshua feeling unaccountably wary.

A plump lady of middle years joined the infantry, soon followed by a tallish man in a greatcoat, but no hat.

"Mama! Joshua! Look! I have cousins! For Christmas this year, I have cousins and an Auntie Alma and an Uncle Orson, and we played hide-and-seek and ate stollen and sang the wrong words and everything!"

"You have company," Joshua said, the wary feeling shifting toward resignation. "You have company, Hope, and I..."

She gaped at the tableau on the porch. "That's Orson and Alma, and the children are half grown, and Holly is so..."

Joshua passed her a handkerchief, directed the footman to retrieve the baked goods, and kissed Hope's cheek.

"You have family, Hope. I will finish up at the bank. I'll send the footman around to the chophouse for some comestibles, and you can catch up with your family in my absence."

Before Hope could reply, the largish lady approached at a purposeful trot, her arms outstretched, the whole group on the terrace swarming after her.

"Hope, oh dearest Hope, it has been too long!"

As Hope was thronged with hugs and borne into the house on cascades of laughter, Joshua gave the footman directions, climbed into the vehicle, and instructed the coachy to head back to the bank.

~

"Mrs. Burdette, good day." Joshua rose from his desk, looking tall, fit, exquisitely turned out, and utterly businesslike. His desk was twice the size of the one at the house and intricately inlaid along the edges.

Hope would bet her sewing basket that no cat had ever sat, licking its paws, on that tooled leather blotter.

The whole office exuded good taste, from the plush floral carpets to the perfectly draped green velvet curtains, to the deeply cushioned wing chairs next to the merrily blazing hearth.

Though Hope would have added some camellias cheerfully blooming on the sideboard. And to think Joshua had slept on that lumpy sofa...

"This is a pleasant surprise," he said, though the reserve in his tone would pleasantly have frozen the Thames. "Might I take your wrap?"

"You may not, and you may keep for all time your polite little invitation to discuss a rental agreement." Hope brandished the offending epistle, which had arrived on the third day of the New Year. If Hope survived until sunset, the evening would see the arrival of Twelfth Night, the final hurrah of the long holiday season.

"My invitation?"

"Holiday greetings to me and my household," Hope retorted, "by which I assume you meant Heifer and Holly. You state an availability at my convenience to discuss real estate matters as yet unresolved." *Respectfully, Joshua Penrose.*

"I am happy to call upon you at the house, and the matter is not urgent. Shall we make an appointment?"

She could read nothing in his question. Not curiosity, boredom, eagerness to be rid of her, or pleasure in her company. He was once again the half-frozen stranger she'd met on that frigid, snowy night nearly a fortnight ago.

"Now suits me very conveniently, Mr. Penrose, and I'm here to tell you that you may keep your house. I know it means a great deal to you, and it's been in your family for some time. I never meant to see you homeless."

"Lord Stephen is putting me up for the nonce. He dwells in a bachelor's version of luxury, though he keeps very irregular hours." Joshua gestured to the wing chairs. "Shall we sit?"

At least he didn't intend to put her before his desk like some penitent at the altar of finance. "Her Grace worries about Lord Stephen," Hope said. "She says his brooding casts the duke's efforts in the same direction in the shade."

Surprise flickered through Joshua's politely arranged features. "You have made Her Grace's acquaintance?"

Hope took a seat in a chair so comfortable, it begged for good books and full tea trays. "The duchess called on me just as I was going out to call on her. I like her very much, and she is worried about you."

"She worries about you too." Joshua took the second wing chair. "If you notice a dapper, dark-haired fellow occasionally chatting up Slivers or one of the other crossing sweepers, that will be Mr. Edward Wentworth, affectionately known as Ned, whose acquaintance you have made. He is her elf, minion, and vassal-at-large."

"I haven't any elves worth the name at present, hence I am calling on you myself. Holly assumes our presence is what's preventing you from coming home. She thinks we should go live with Alma and Orson."

Joshua drummed his nails in a steady one-two-three-four-pause, one-two-three-four-pause rhythm on the arm of the chair, then stopped himself.

"You must dwell wherever it pleases you to dwell. I don't want the house back, Hope. I thought when I returned to London... I thought being under that roof would help put the past to rest, but instead... I can deed it to Holly if you'd like to keep it in trust for her. I will also sell it to you very reasonably, if you insist on paying for it. You have only to say what you want."

I want you, you dunderheaded man. Why was it so hard to put that into words? Though Hope knew why. Anybody who'd loved and lost knew the potential dangers of loving again.

Of living again. "You truly won't reside there?"

He rose to toss another square of peat on the fire, dusted his hands, and remained on his feet.

"You are right when you say it's too big. The house was built for show, to prove to all of London that the Penroses were a formidable banking family, or something. I am not a formidable banking family. I am just... me. Why heat all those rooms? Why keep staff running up and down six different staircases for one man?"

"You've been pondering this." And honestly, Hope did not like to think of him rattling around that vast edifice without even a cat for company.

He scrubbed a hand over his face and resumed his seat. "Ned says the holidays require courage of us, and in the manner of the proverbial blind hog, he's come close to the mark. *Celebrating* the holidays, or a child's first tooth, or some grandmama's eightieth natal day requires courage. I enjoyed Christmas with you and Holly very much. Perhaps too much."

"What are you going on about?"

He smiled wanly. "I should have rehearsed a pretty speech, but Stephen claims rehearsed speeches show a lack of confidence. I have recently had the benefit of many expert opinions, you see. May I speak plainly, Hope?"

"We have always been honest with each other." Hope braced herself for an admission that the whole Yuletide encounter had been a lovely mistake, an understandable wrong turn for two people coping with many challenges. Whatever the words were, Joshua would know them and deliver them with gently implacable finesse.

All the gingerbread in the world would be no comfort whatsoever in the face of his rejection.

"It's just a house," he said slowly. "A big house full of nice things, but until I shared it with you, it was not a home. Until we rejoiced together to find a lot of stinky old coal hiding in the conservatory, until you smiled at me over the kitchen table, until... well. I will keep the memories with me always, but the house itself can be put to a better use if you don't want it."

"Heifer has taken to sleeping on your sofa," Hope said, apropos of absolutely nothing. "I think he's guarding it for you."

"And Holly?"

"She wanted me to tell you that her cousins are gone, and it's safe to come home now. I told her... When you did not return to the house, I told Holly it was because you didn't want to intrude on our other company. Then Alma and Orson decamped, and the house is too quiet, and you sent that blasted note. Holly's cousins have shown her a new way to polish the bannisters that is beyond anything."

"Hope—"

"Joshua—" She had never seen him look so solemn. "You first."

"I miss you," he said simply. "I miss hearing your footsteps up in the parlor while I'm oiling my boots in the kitchen. I miss seeing you tending a skillet full of bacon and looking utterly expert at it. I miss your quick hugs and your slow smiles. I miss you in a way I wish was impossible, but there it is every waking hour. All missing and no you."

Not a rehearsed speech, but certainly not a rejection either. "I miss your innuendos and bungled lyrics," Hope said. "I miss your patience with Holly and how you are never too busy to indulge me in a hug. I miss the sight of you across the breakfast table, and the..."

"Hope?"

"The pleasure of you in the dark." An understatement. "But you look so bankerish now and so, so... unlike my Joshua. I want to shake you and kiss you and... Perhaps I should leave."

Joshua put a hand on her arm. "When Jane refers to His Grace as bankerish, she is not paying him a compliment. If I appear on my dignity, that's because I am unsure of myself."

"I don't like feeling unsure. I've had enough of that to last me a lifetime. I know who and what I want, Joshua Penrose of the Banking Penroses."

He offered her his hand, and Hope took it.

"I know as well, madam, but one doesn't dare presume. I want to court you, Hope, and ask Holly's permission to pay you my addresses. I'll ask your brother as well, if you like, but you seem quite able to speak for yourself. I want us to share a roof, of course, but Grandpapa's house is mostly going to waste."

"Not according to Gabriel and his friends. They have made the conservatory over into a sort of dormitory, though everything is all put away and tidied up in the morning."

"More about those scamps later." Joshua did not adopt a kneeling posture, but he enclosed Hope's hand in both of his. "Please, may I court you, Hope Burdette? You have no need of my money or my house or my anything, but I love you, and nothing and no one will ever change that."

Hope rose and arranged herself in his lap. "I love you, too, and I would like to be courted—briefly—if that's how you want to proceed. Alma and Orson wrote to me, you know. They weren't aware of Edwin's passing, until an old mutual acquaintance mentioned it. Orson had been writing to Peters, whom he knew to be Edwin's solicitor, and you can guess the rest. Years of silence between family members just so Peters could swindle me out of a fortune."

"He has already booked passage for Paris." Joshua spoke against her temple. "Plodgely owns the entire shop, and Peters is having to sell his lovely home to pay what he owes to several of his clients."

"That report makes my New Year very happy. I would like a cozy house, Joshua. Nothing fancy."

His lips gently grazed her brow. "The fancy house can be made over as a clerks' academy. I've put the question to Ned, who is a great one for taking on projects and a former ne'er-do-well himself. Reformed, of course. Our house will be comfortable and have only comfortable art."

"No samplers."

"No samplers, unless Holly chooses to grace us with a few, and you must promise me never to put anise biscuits on our holiday menu and never to volunteer me to play a shepherd in any Christmas pageants."

The experts weighing in again, no doubt. "Your friend Ned enjoys a unique perspective. We'll have the boys to tea when they've worked on their manners a bit."

"Or worked on them a lot, and we can visit Orson and Alma as often as you like." He kissed her forehead and sighed, tickling her ear.

"Our cozy house will have a big garden," Hope said. No conservatory, though. A garden was much better than a conservatory.

"A big enough garden that Heifer will think himself king of the jungle."

Hope snuggled closer. "Then, yes. I will marry you, and we will sing all the wrong words at Yuletide, and stuff ourselves with warm gingerbread, and have such a cozy house where nobody who comes to call on us is ever cold."

"And mistletoe," Joshua said, an audible gleam illuminating his words. "Buckets and bales of mistletoe."

Hope took hold of Joshua around the neck and set about explaining to him that mistletoe at the holidays—at any time of year—was completely unnecessary when two determined parties were intent on a particular variety of celebration.

They named Holly's little sister Ivy and Ivy's twin brother Nicholas, and the cozy house was sometimes a noisy cozy house, but it was above all a happy, loving home for all who dwelled under its roof.

Printed in Dunstable, United Kingdom

83085401R00080